ABOUT THE AUTHOR

Jane Peart, award-winning novelist and short story writer, grew up in Asheville, North Carolina, and was educated in New England. Although she now lives in northern California, her heart has remained in her native South—its people, its history, and its traditions. With more than twenty-five novels and 250 short stories to her credit, Jane likes to emphasize in her writing the timeless and recurring themes of family, traditional values, and a sense of place.

Ten years in the writing, the *Brides of Montclair* series is a historical family saga of enduring beauty. In each new book, another generation comes into its own at the beautiful Montclair estate near Williamsburg, Virginia. These compelling, dramatic stories reaffirm the importance of committed love, loyalty, courage, strength of character, and abiding faith in times of triumph and tragedy, sorrow and joy.

Hero's Bride

Book Eleven
The Brides of Montclair Series

JANE PEART

ZondervanPublishingHouse
Grand Rapids, Michigan

A Division of HarperCollinsPublishers

Hero's Bride
Copyright © 1993 by Jane Peart

Requests for information should be addressed to:
Zondervan Publishing House
Grand Rapids, Michigan 49530

Library of Congress Cataloging-in-Publication Data

Peart, Jane.
    Hero's bride / Jane Peart.
       p. cm. — (The Brides of Montclair series : bk. 11)
    ISBN 0-310-67141-8 (paper)
    1. Family—Virginia—Williamsburg Region—Fiction. 2. Williams-
burg Region (Va.)—Fiction. I. Title. II. Series: Peart, Jane. Brides of
Montclair series : bk. 11.
    PS3566.E238H4   1993
    813'.54—dc20   93-19162
                                                                CIP

Edited by Anne Severance
Interior design by Kim Koning
Cover design by Art Jacobs
Cover illustration by Wes Lowe, Sal Baracc and Assoc., Inc.

Printed in the United States of America

93 94 95 96 97 98 99 00 01 / LP / 10 9 8 7 6 5 4 3 2 1

This book is gratefully dedicated to
Bob Hudson,
senior editor at Zondervan,
in appreciation for his supportive encouragement,
his enthusiasm and help

Hero's Bride

Prologue

August 1914

From: Katherine M. Cameron
       Cameron Hall
       Mayfield, Virginia

To: Mrs. Owen Brandt
       Good Shepherd Parsonage
       Harristown, Ohio

Dearest Twin,

The events of this past month are unreal, aren't they? Just a few weeks ago, Lynette and I were at Birchfields visiting Aunt Garnet in the peaceful English countryside, and now England is at war with Germany.

Mama is terribly upset. You know she lived in England for nearly ten years before coming back to Virginia and marrying Daddy, and still has lots of friends there. She has also traveled in Germany and remembers it as such a beautiful place, famous for its music and culture.

But she is mostly concerned because of Bryanne. She keeps saying that she wishes I'd brought her back with us when Lynette and I returned in June. But you know Aunt Garnet, Cara. She wouldn't hear of it. She said that one child was enough of a responsibility for me on a long ocean voyage and that she would bring Brynnie over herself later. Of course, that's out of the question now. With the Germans prowling the high seas, Aunt Garnet says it's much too dangerous to think of crossing the Atlantic.

As if that weren't all Mama had to worry about, Jeff still refuses to come back from New Mexico. Mama thinks Gareth should be in a more normal home situation, not living with a widowed father in an art colony. She thinks it's very bad for these three motherless children to be growing up in separate homes, under entirely different circumstances. How can they ever feel like a family again?

She's probably right. Brynnie has already acquired an English accent. Can you believe *that*?

It's hard to understand why these things happen, isn't it? How everyone could be so happy one minute, and the next, ripped apart by a tragic accident like the sinking of the *Titanic*. Remember how we used to think that Jeff and Faith and their children lived a kind of fairy-tale existence at Avalon? It was almost Camelot come to life.

How does Owen explain such things? As a minister, he ought to have more insight into the problem of pain in innocent lives than we do.

I still find it hard to think of you as a minister's wife, Cara. I just never imagined you teaching Sunday school and chairing the Ladies' Guild. I guess nobody else did, either. But when you said you'd follow Owen to the ends of the earth, I guess you meant it. Still, it's a good thing it was just to a little rural town in Ohio in a small country parish, not Africa, isn't it?

What did you think of the news that Jonathan and Phoebe Montrose have a baby boy? Kip seemed stunned that his father is starting another family. The christening was last Sunday—a lovely party at Montclair—and the baby is darling. They've named him Fraser, after Phoebe's oldest brother. Of course, she is disappointed that they had to call off their trip to Scotland because of the war. Also, she's worried about her nephews, all at an age for military service.

Things are as usual here. We miss you always. I don't think I'll ever get used to the idea of not having you near to talk things over with, or to wake up in the mornings and not see you in the next bed.

But I do know how happy you are, so that makes me happy, too.

Love, Kitty

Part I
Blue Skies

Mayfield, Virginia
Autumn 1914

Blue skies, smilin' at me,
Nothin' but blue skies do I see . . .
—a popular song

chapter
1

SUMMER FLOWED gently into fall, after lingering longer than usual in the Virginia countryside. The days were brilliant still, but darkness came more quickly now.

This autumn the colors were dazzling, the elms that lined the driveway up to Cameron Hall were golden against the dark green pines of the surrounding woods, the dogwoods were ruby-red and the maples on the lawn were butter-bright tinged with crimson. The gardens too were ablaze—saffron-yellow, russet, and amber chrysanthemums glistened like jewels in the September sunshine.

This was her favorite time of year, Kitty Cameron decided as she bent over her plants in one of the flower beds. Out in the crisp fall air, the combination of scents—ripening fruit in the orchards, distant wood smoke, the rich smell of earth—was exhilarating. Even the mundane chore of digging up tulip and gladiola bulbs for winter storage gave her enormous pleasure.

Rod Cameron, coming out onto the columned porch of the stately Georgian house that had been his family's home for generations, caught sight of his daughter. He stood at the edge of the steps and watched her work, her expression one of total concentration.

After a moment he strolled over, pausing beside her. "Must be in the genes."

Kitty smiled up at him. "Well, I *was* named for Grandmother, wasn't I?"

It was a family joke that Kitty's love of gardening must have been inherited from Katherine Cameron, who, in spite of having at least four gardeners at Cameron Hall during its "glory days," had insisted on doing much of her own work.

Looking into his daughter's upturned face, Rod was startled by a fresh recognition of how pretty she was. The sun, glinting on her auburn hair, enriched its vibrancy. One strand fell forward, and she brushed it back with an impatient gesture that left a smudge of dirt on her cheek. Her long-lashed eyes were softly brown, like his adored wife's. But where Blythe's face revealed the deep contentment of a long and happy marriage, there was something vulnerable about Kitty's that tugged at her father's heart.

He had tried to give his daughters everything possible to assure their well-being, but the one thing he had never been able to give them was happiness, so often found in unexpected places. Cara, Kitty's twin, was a prime example. She'd found hers in marriage to a penniless preacher! Unconsciously, Rod sighed. Impetuous and independent as she was, he missed Cara.

Turning his attention to Kitty again, he remarked, "I suppose you're right. As they say, 'blood will tell.'" Then with a wave he walked away, striding down the gravel drive toward the stables.

Kitty's glance followed his tall figure. Except for the slight limp, a token reminder of the wound he'd acquired during the War Between the States, her father appeared much younger than his sixty-odd years. He was still handsome with strong, aristocratic features, thick gray hair, an erect bearing.

Recalling her father's teasing, Kitty cast a brief look at the metal marker verdigrised with age, placed among the rose-bushes years before by her grandmother and read the quotation: "The kiss of the sun for pardon,/the song of the birds for mirth,/You are nearer God's heart in a garden/Than anywhere else on earth." It spoke of her serene spirit, and Kitty was glad once again to be considered very like the other Katherine.

She returned to her digging, working steadily until she heard the sound of a motorcar roaring up the drive. *Kip,* she guessed, even before she saw the shiny green roadster round the bend of the driveway and pull up in front of the house, scattering gravel stones as he braked.

Kitty sat back on her heels and waved to him. "Good morning!"

Kip Montrose gave her an answering wave, then vaulted over the door of his open runabout and started over to join her.

At his approach, Kitty's heart flip-flopped foolishly. It happened every time, no matter how hard she tried to control herself. Everything about Kip—his saunter, the roguish smile, his tousled dark hair, the mischievous twinkle in his eyes—caused this ridiculous reaction.

Kitty felt her face grow warm. She ducked her head, pulled up a bulb, and pretended to focus on shaking the dirt from its root. "What are you doing up and about this early?" she asked with studied casualness.

"I'm about to let you in on a secret," he teased, grinning down at her.

Kitty looked skeptical. "What kind of secret?"

"What do you mean *what kind*? A secret's just that, a secret," he retorted. "Come on, 'Mary, Mary,' don't be contrary. Let your garden grow on its own for a while. I want to take you someplace."

"Oh, Kip, I can't," she protested. "I'm right in the middle of all this."

"Let it go," Kip demanded impatiently. "Come on, Kitty. Making mud pies can wait. This is important."

"And what I'm doing *isn't?*"

"Not as important as what I'm about to show you."

"Why are you being so mysterious? Why don't you just tell me? Let me decide—"

"Trust me, Kitty. Come on."

Slowly she dragged off her gardening gloves and brushed her skirt. Thrilled as she was that Kip wanted to whisk her away with him, she didn't want to appear too eager, ready to drop everything at his spur-of-the-moment invitation.

Feigning reluctance, she said, "Well . . . I'll have to change—"

"For Pete's sake, Kitty, you don't have to change!" Kip sounded exasperated. He grabbed her hand and pulled her to her feet. "You look fine. Just dandy."

Puzzled at his insistence, Kitty hung back. "Wait, Kip. I *do* have to tell Mother I'm leaving."

"All right. But hurry! We don't have all day!"

Kitty threw Kip a reproving look as she hurried past him, up the terrace steps and into the house. Kip was used to having his own way. She really shouldn't accommodate him so easily, she reminded herself. But, as usual, she didn't have the will to resist.

Inside, Kitty went to find her mother. Blythe was in her sitting room at her desk when Kitty stuck her head in the door and told her she was going for a drive with Kip.

Unbuttoning the brown canvas gardening smock, Kitty flung it on a chair and grabbed a cardigan sweater from the coat tree in the hall. With one hasty peek in the mirror, she gave an ineffectual pat to her hair, then ran out the front door and down the steps.

Kip was already behind the driver's seat, looking as if he were about to hit the horn. Seeing her, he reached over and opened the door on the passenger side.

"Where are we going?" she asked as they started off.

"You'll see."

At the end of the driveway, Kip shifted down and made a sharp turn onto the country road. They were soon bumping over the ruts at some speed. Hunched over the wheel, Kip was curiously intent on his driving, with none of his usual irritated comments about the road conditions or "Why didn't the county fund paving now with so many motor vehicles about!" Instead, he seemed wound up as if with suppressed excitement.

Suddenly, he jammed on the brakes and spun the wheel to the left, sending the vehicle bouncing down a lane that seemed hardly more than a cow path.

"Slow down, Kip, for goodness sake!" Kitty pleaded. "My teeth are being shaken out of my head!"

"Sorry, Kit! It's only a bit farther now."

"But where? This looks like a dead end to me."

Just ahead was a cattle gate. Kip slammed the brake pedal, then jerked the hand brake. Jumping out of the car, he walked over to open the gate and swing it wide. In a flash he was sliding under the wheel again, and they proceeded into an open field.

"Kip! We can't drive through here!"

"Don't worry, Kitty. It's all right."

She gripped the armrest as they plowed ahead over the uneven ground. Then straight in front of them she saw a large cleared space in the middle of the meadow. A few makeshift, weather-beaten sheds and a large barn-like structure stood at the end.

Kip brought the car to an abrupt stop and announced triumphantly, "Here we are!"

"Here we are ... *where?*"

"Bell Park Flying Field."

"*Flying* field?" she echoed. "I don't understand."

"You will." Kip got out of the car. "Come see."

Kitty remained where she was, bewildered as to why he had brought her to this deserted place. While she was still wondering, the barn door slid back and a lanky man in coveralls emerged, wiping his hands on an oily rag as he walked out into the sunshine.

Kip waved and shouted to him. "Hiyah, Beau!"

"How's yourself, Kip?"

The two greeted each other like old friends. Kitty was puzzled as she observed them. She thought she knew most of Kip's friends, but this man was a stranger to her. Finally, as if remembering her, Kip jerked his head in her direction, and together they strolled back to the car.

Offhandedly, Kip introduced them. "Beau Chartyrs. Kitty Cameron."

At closer range, Kitty could see that the other man, in spite of his grease-smudged face, was quite good-looking. He grinned.

"Nice to meet you. Kip said he was going to bring you out soon."

The idea that Kip had discussed her with this stranger puzzled Kitty even more. Who was this fellow? And what was going on here?

"So, how's it going?" Kip asked Beau.

"She's a sweet little bird." Beau smiled. "I took her up this

20

morning, and the engine's purring like a kitten." He paused, then asked, "I gather you want to take 'er up yourself, right?"

Kitty turned a startled gaze on Kip. He met it, his own eyes shining.

"You—you're going to *fly?*" Kitty was incredulous.

"Sure thing. I've been taking flying lessons for six weeks or more. In fact, I'm almost ready to take my test for a certificate to become a licensed pilot."

"Does your father know?"

"Not yet. Anyway, you're the only one I've told. So now you're in on the secret and can't say a word until I give you the green light." He fixed her with a fierce glare.

"Kip, that's not fair."

"Now, Kitty, don't turn all righteous on me. Besides, I wanted *you* to be the first to know, to see for yourself." He turned to Beau. "All set? Then let's go. Now, Kitty, this is a two-seater. Beau's an experienced pilot and he's going along . . . just in case—"

"Just in case of *what?*" she gasped.

"Don't worry, Miss Cameron. Kip's a natural," Beau reassured her. "He'll be fine."

Speechless, Kitty watched as the two men pushed the airplane out from the barn with the help of an even grubbier fellow in grease-spotted coveralls whom Kip called Mike. Then Kip shrugged into a leather jacket, donned a helmet-like cap, and after giving her a broad wink, pulled goggles down over his eyes and climbed into the front cockpit of the flimsy-looking little plane.

Beau clambered into the rear seat and signaled to Mike, who ran around in front and started spinning the propeller. It made such a roar that Kitty had to cover her ears.

She stood rigidly as the winged vehicle wobbled over the uneven grass down to the end of the field and made an uncertain turn. Then, before her eyes and with the engines making a huge racket, it began to race down the cleared path, faster and faster, until it lifted from the ground into the air.

"Oh, dear Lord!" she prayed aloud, clasping her hands tightly together in a heartfelt prayer.

Running out behind them, she followed the ascent of the plane as it climbed higher and higher into the blue September sky. Even as she tracked its progress, the plane seemed to be swallowed up in the clouds and finally disappeared from sight.

It all seemed like some kind of dream. When the two young men returned from their flight, Beau congratulating Kip on achieving a perfect landing, Kitty was still trying to take it all in. On the way back to Cameron Hall, she rode in shocked silence.

With the sinking of the *Lusitania* by a German submarine, in May 1915, all the tragedy and horror the two families had suffered in the *Titanic* disaster was brought vividly to mind.

The incident also served to point up the Germans' willful disregard of the basic rules of civilized warfare, the wanton pursuit of their power goals despite loss of innocent lives. Their determination to conduct unrestricted and intensified submarine warfare, regardless of neutral rights, persisted. The fact that 127 Americans had perished brought the United States closer to entering the European war on the side of the Allies. President Wilson, however, still refused to commit.

Kip was incensed. At the little café at the airfield, he and Beau discussed world affairs endlessly. "It makes me ashamed to be an American!"

Kitty was shocked. "Oh, Kip, you don't mean that!"

"Well, I *do!* Look, we owe France. *They* came in, sent men, money, volunteers to help us in our War of Independence, didn't they? It might even have been the turning point. The

British could have won! We might still be a British colony today if it hadn't been for France!" Kip banged his fist on the rickety table, causing their mugs to dance.

Beau, of course, agreed with Kip. But Kitty did not feel she knew enough about the situation to venture an opinion. She didn't want to take the opposite viewpoint from Kip on an issue that was so important to him. On the other hand, she had heard her father speak out strongly against America's intervention in a foreign war.

"It would be reckless and irresponsible for us to go in. President Wilson is right," Rod had said firmly. "Nothing is worth risking the lives of thousands of young men. Why can't people remember our own terrible war, the deep scars that have still not been erased? Any man who survived that bitter experience should applaud the President's decision." Rod added proudly—"You *know* he's a *Virginian!*"

Kitty knew, too, that there had also been opposing opinions about the war her father had served in. That war had pitted brother against brother, husband against wife. Whole families had been torn asunder over it. Kip's own grandfather and grandmother, Malcom Montrose and his wife, Rose, had been sadly estranged over the right and wrong of that war. She wasn't about to jeopardize her tenuous relationship with Kip by debating the issue!

So Kitty remained silent. War was a man's business. Men made war, fought wars. That's the way it had always been.

chapter
2

July 2, 1915

Dearest Twin,

Just a short note to tell you I'm taking Lynette to Cape Cod to visit Meredith. She's written so many times begging me to come for a visit, but there always seemed something to prevent my going. Last year, of course, I took Lynette to England to see her little sister at Aunt Garnet's. Now, with the war going into its second year, there's no telling when those two children will get to see each other again.

Mama has been real concerned about Lynette. She does seem sad sometimes, even though we all do everything we know to keep her happy and content. Father has been wonderful, has taken a real interest in teaching her to ride, and Lynette is doing quite well. She will soon be graduating from her beloved pony to a horse he has hand-picked for her.

Anyway, when Merry's last invitation came, it was decided that it would be good for Lynette to have a change of scene and that the sea air would do her a world of good. Summer is the best time for Merry to have us come, since Manuel is out on his fishing boat two and three days at a time, and she writes that she "longs for company." She is thrilled to have Lynette come, too, and says there are lots of children nearby to keep her company.

Remember our summer at Fair Winds? Well, of course you do! That's the summer you met Owen. I'll write from there, but I don't expect to hear from you. I know you're busy with Vacation Bible School. Good luck!

Love always, Kitty

When Kitty told Kip about her plans, he seemed not only surprised but angry.

"For the whole summer?"

"Not quite. A month or six weeks, actually."

"That's crazy! What in the world do you want to do that for!" he demanded.

"Kip! I don't understand why you're so upset. Merry's your own sister and my very best friend!"

"Well, but . . . why do you have to be gone so long?"

"For one thing, I haven't seen Merry in months, and we'll have a wonderful time together."

"Doing what?"

"What we always do at the Cape—swim, walk on the beach, *talk!* We have lots to catch up on."

Kip plunged his hands into his jacket pocket, pouting like a small boy. "Talk? For six weeks? That's ridiculous!"

"You don't understand. Men just don't." Kitty smiled and shrugged.

They were standing below the steps of Cameron Hall. Kip had just driven Kitty home from the airfield where they had spent most of the afternoon. Kip had been practicing landings and Kitty had sat in the little café, drinking coffee and holding her breath as she watched him.

"So, when are you leaving?" Kip asked.

"Next week."

"So soon?" Again he seemed offended. "Why didn't you tell me?"

"Kip, I'm sure I must have mentioned it. You just weren't listening."

He frowned, then said doubtfully, "I don't think so, or I'd have remembered—"

Kitty had to laugh. "Oh, Kip, your head is in the clouds so much of the time, you don't hear half of what's said to you!"

He gave her a doleful glance. "I'm going to miss you."

She shook her head. "No, you won't. You'll be too busy flying, taking engines apart with Beau."

"You're wrong, Kitty. I'm used to having you with me, riding out to the field with me, being there when I land and climb out of the cockpit. It means a lot to me that you understand, that you don't fuss or nag about it being dangerous or silly . . . which, of course, it isn't—" He paused, put both hands on her shoulders and stared down into her eyes. "Kitty, don't you know how special you are to me?"

With all her heart, Kitty wished Kip meant what he was saying. But deep down, she didn't believe he cared for her in the same way she cared for him. Not yet. Maybe he never would. She shouldn't put too much meaning into his words.

Sure, she was "special" to him. She was the one who had given him the proverbial shoulder to cry on when Cara left him for Owen, the one who sympathized, listened, bolstered his self-esteem, and encouraged him. She had comforted him when his mother had died so tragically on the *Titanic,* and tried to support him when he groped for new meaning in his life. She had been his friend. And she was wise enough to realize that "friend" might be all she would ever be to Kip.

Afraid she might betray her deeper feelings, Kitty leaned up and gave him a light kiss.

"And *you* are very special to me, Kip."

Then, with a casual wave, she turned and ran up the steps and into the house.

Besides, it might do Kip good to *really* miss her while she was gone. That is, if that old adage, "absence makes the heart grow fonder," is true!

chapter

3

Nantucket Island, Mass.

Summer 1915

THE CAPE SEEMED another world away, unchanged despite the seven years that had passed since Kitty and Cara had spent that last enchanted summer here. It even smelled the same—the salty tang of the sea air, the sharp aroma of geraniums spilling out of window boxes along the main street of town, the clean, wind-swept breeze.

Fair weather held long after Kitty's arrival with Lynette in tow, and they quickly settled into the leisurely pace of life in the Sousa house—a quaint sea-silvered "salt-box," as neat and orderly as Merry herself. Beyond a piled-rock fence, they could see the dunes, the dark blue ocean breaking in frothy foam onto the beach.

Occasionally Kitty felt a sad little twinge, aware that she had not yet found what both Cara and her friend had found—love given and returned in full measure. For Merry was lyrical about her darkly handsome Portuguese husband, Manuel, and the dimpled baby boy who filled her life.

A professional fisherman, Manny was usually up by dawn

and out on his father's fishing boat before the household stirred. And since his work sometimes took him away for two or three days at a time, Meredith and Kitty had plenty of time alone together.

Their days took on a pleasant pattern. Before noon, they took the baby in his carriage, a beach umbrella, blankets, and a picnic basket down to the beach. There was no lack of playmates for Lynette, for here other families from the cottages fronting the ocean gathered to while away the summer hours.

While the baby napped and Lynette joined her new friends to build sandcastles, search for shells, or wade near the shore, Meredith and Kitty had a chance to catch up on all the years since that enchanted summer.

Their long friendship dated back to childhood, and there had been few secrets between them. Meredith had sensed Kitty's love for Kip before Kitty was even willing to admit it to herself. Now they spoke freely about the things closest to their hearts.

"If Kip doesn't wake up and realize it soon, someone else will, Kitty!" Meredith declared. "You're much too special for someone not to fall madly in love with you and carry you off soon. *Then* my brother will be sorry!"

"You can't *make* someone love you, Merry. Kip thinks of me as a friend, someone he enjoys being with, someone he can trust. He doesn't think of me romantically at all—" She paused, then said haltingly, "I'm not sure he's ever gotten over losing Cara. Maybe he never will—"

Meredith shook her head. "That would never have worked, even if Cara had wanted it to. They were too much alike. Mama always said they were like flint and stone. Whenever they were together, sparks flew. Imagine what kind of a marriage that would have been!"

Kitty smiled pensively. Distracted for the moment by the shouts and shrieks of laughter on the shore where the children were splashing and rolling in the shallow waves, she did not reply to Merry's comment.

After nearly a month of sunshine came two days of overcast skies, rain, and high winds. The beaches were deserted, the ocean turbulent.

On one such afternoon, Lynette was invited over to play with some little friends at another cottage. While Merry was rocking Jonny to sleep, Kitty found herself alone in the small sitting room. Browsing through the bookcase for something to read, she came upon a photograph album. Reading its label, SUMMER 1908, she felt a clutching sensation in her heart. That was the summer they had all been together at Fair Winds, the rambling Victorian beach house that belonged to Meredith's grandfather, Colonel Kendall Carpenter. That summer held all sorts of memories for Kitty.

Curious, Kitty sat down on the floor, drew it from the shelf, and onto her lap. Almost reluctantly, she opened it. In Meredith's methodical manner, each snapshot was fastened in place by tiny black corners. Underneath, neatly printed in white ink, was the name, identifying the person in the picture and the date it was taken.

One of the first pictures Kitty came across was of herself and her twin, wearing identical middy blouses, sailor collars and ties, and pleated skirts, their hair whipped by the breeze off the ocean behind them. Looking at those laughing faces brought a lump into Kitty's throat. That had been the time when she and Cara had begun to tread their own paths, to find their separate selves. It was the summer of Cara's secret romance with Owen Brandt. Kitty could still feel the sting of that first separation, the first time her twin had ever shut her out of an important event. She was surprised to find that it still hurt.

There was a group picture of all the young people who had vacationed at the Cape that summer, several of them in makeshift costumes donned for one of the amateur theatricals they'd put on. As she studied that one, Kitty saw something she had failed to see at the time. Everyone was facing straight ahead, looking at the camera, except Owen and Cara. They were gazing at each other with such rapt expressions on their faces that a person would have had to be blind not to see that they were in love! But of course Kitty *had* been blinded by her own infatuation with Kip, so she was as surprised as anyone else when the truth came out.

Turning the page, she came upon a snapshot that made her heart stand still. Someone had snapped a picture of Kip in the sailboat. He was wearing a cable-knit sweater, his dark hair wind-tossed, his eyes squinted into the sun. There was that grin she loved so much—the white teeth, the tanned face. As she gazed at it hungrily, she saw another print of the same picture among several loose snapshots not yet pasted onto the page.

After a split-second's hesitation, Kitty picked it up and slipped it into her skirt pocket, telling herself that surely no one would miss it.

The first of August, Kitty left for New York City to be a bridesmaid in the wedding of a college chum, Babs Wescott, and her fiancé, Phil Bennett. Lynette was to stay with Meredith while Kitty spent a week on Long Island for the pre-nuptial parties and other festivities. After that, she would return to the Cape and she and Lynette would take the train back to Virginia in time for the beginning of school.

Lynette was delighted to extend her vacation, and Kitty

went off to meet another member of the wedding party in Boston. When she returned for Lynette, they knew at last that summer was over.

"I'm going to miss you both so much!" Meredith told them. "And I don't know what Jonny will do without his nanny." She took Lynette's face in both her hands and kissed the child's cheeks affectionately.

"Maybe we can come again next summer!" the little girl said hopefully.

"Yes! Please do!" Meredith looked at Kitty over the child's head.

Kitty hugged her friend. "Thanks for everything."

"I wish you'd let me give that brother of mine some sisterly advice," Meredith whispered.

"Don't, please. It's no good unless it's *his* idea."

"Can I help it if I want you for my *real* sister?"

Kitty sighed. "If it's to be, it will be," she replied. "I don't want it any other way."

Kitty got off the train at the Mayfield station a few days later and found Kip pacing the platform impatiently. When he saw her, he was beside her in an instant.

Before she had a chance to say "Hello," he was demanding, "Why did you stay so long? I mean, the wedding was two weeks ago, wasn't it? What were you doing so long in New York?"

Kitty's heart swelled with happiness. Then he *had* missed her! She had not dared think he would, busy as he was every day with his flying, tinkering with his obsession, the little plane he had dubbed "Bonnie Doon."

"I was doing some shopping . . . see?" She twirled about to show off the smart linen suit, touching the narrow brim of her braided silk hat.

33

"You look mighty fashionable, I admit. But you couldn't have spent all your time in stores. They do *close* at night, don't they?"

"Well, we went to some shows, too. Thax had tickets to the new Marilyn Miller revue—"

"Thax?" He scowled darkly.

"Thaxton Collinwood. You know him. A friend of Scott's and Phil's. He was one of the groomsmen in the wedding," Kitty explained. "He and Phil were roommates . . ."

"Oh, yes, I remember," he conceded, not too graciously. "He's a cousin of the Langleys, right?"

Could Kip possibly be jealous?

"Then we went to a *thé dansant*—that's an afternoon dance party to us provincials." Kitty laughed teasingly. "Babs's aunt gave one for the members of the wedding party at the posh Pierre Hotel. They're all the rage in New York now, and—"

Kip held up a restraining hand. "All right, enough! I don't need an itemized list of your social activities. I'm just glad you're back and we can get on with our life."

Our life? Kitty wondered just what Kip meant by that.

"Where's Lynette?" he asked, looking around as if he had just remembered the little girl.

"Mama met us in Richmond. She's taken Lynette to buy school clothes. Wait till you see her. She's grown a foot and is as brown as a berry."

"Well, then, I guess we're all set. I told your father I'd meet you and drive you home."

They were walking down the platform when Kip suddenly halted. "I've missed you like blazes, Kitty."

She bit her lower lip to control the surge of pleasure at his words. "Thanks, Kip. It's nice to know that one is missed."

When they reached the end of the platform, Kitty saw the

little green car parked at the curb. Kip opened the door on the passenger side and stood there absentmindedly.

"Kip, my bags—" she reminded him gently.

"Sorry, I forgot. Had something else on my mind. Wait here. I'll be right back."

Kitty laughed. "Of course, I'll wait! Where would I go?"

Kip was back within minutes, tossed her suitcase and hatbox into the back with abandon, and slid behind the wheel.

"Kitty, we've got to talk," Kip said firmly, shoving the car into gear and backing out of the parking space.

She felt her heart give another leap but spoke as casually as she could manage, "Oh, yes, how's the flying?"

"This is not about flying. It's about us."

"*Us?*" she croaked.

"Yes. You and me, Kitty."

She tried to look surprised, puzzled, but did not succeed. She could feel her lips part in a hopeful smile. "What about us?" she asked in a tremulous voice.

She looked over at Kip, saw the dear, familiar profile, the one she knew by heart. They were past Main Street now, turning onto the county road that led out to their neighboring plantations. Kip made the turn, pressed the accelerator, and they sped along until he made a sudden swerve off into a lane half-concealed by shaggy rhododendron bushes. Pulling on the brake, he stopped the car.

He turned toward her, one arm slid across the back of the leather seat. "You know I love you, Kitty." His eyes searched for some response. "You *do* know that, don't you?"

Kitty nodded slowly, not trusting herself to speak.

He rushed on. "I didn't realize how much until this summer. But it was this past month that I *really* knew. I don't want to be without you again. I don't want to lose you . . .

35

not to Thaxton Collinwood ... not to *anyone*. Marry me, Kitty."

She started to speak but found she couldn't.

Kip reached for her hand. "What do you say?"

If she were smart, she'd hesitate, keep him waiting. But Kitty was much too honest. Besides, her ears ringing with what he had just asked, she felt a surge of joy that could not be denied.

"Kitty?"

Silly tears rushed into her eyes, but she could only nod. Then he took her in his arms and kissed her the way Kitty had long dreamed of being kissed, and she was lost in the ecstasy of the moment.

"Yes, oh yes," she murmured before his mouth covered hers again. She had waited so long for this. "Darling Kip, I love you so."

chapter

4

Winter 1915

Let me call you sweetheart, I'm in love with you,
Let me hear you whisper that you love me, too. . . .

And when I told them, they didn't believe me,
That from this great, big world you've chosen me.
                    —from two popular songs

ON ONE OF THOSE brilliant mornings that come to Virginia in
early fall, each turning leaf—bronze, gold, and russet—
etched sharply against a vivid blue sky, Kip arrived at
Cameron Hall to take Kitty to Bell Park Field.

She had tried desperately to understand Kip's passion for
flying. She knew that he had always been restless, easily
bored, always looking for new challenges. Flying was the new
frontier for the bold, the adventurous, the young explorers. It
suited him, she had to admit. So she had gamely agreed to
accompany him twice a week to the airfield for his flying
lesson.

Today, however, she had other plans for them.

"Let's take a walk first. I have something to show you," Kitty said mysteriously when he appeared on the doorstep.

Uncharacteristically, Kip fell in with the plan, cocking an eyebrow inquisitively but obeying.

She whistled for Shamus, her Irish setter, and they set out down the drive. At the path leading into the woods, the dog took off like a red streak through the brush, then wheeled and bounded back to them before taking off again.

"Can't you tell me where we're going?" Kip asked.

"You'll see."

"I think you're trying to take your revenge," Kip teased.

Kitty did not reply but glanced up at him, eyes twinkling. They walked on quite a distance into the woods before she stopped.

"Close your eyes now. I'll lead you the rest of the way."

"Ah, Kitty, aren't we a little old for 'Blind Man's Bluff'?"

"Just be patient. It's only a little farther now." She took his hand and tugged gently.

They moved forward more slowly now with Kitty in the lead. The deeper they went into the woods, the more peaceful it seemed. Only the rustle of birds in the trees, the faraway sound of the creek rushing to the river, disturbed the deep silence.

When they came to a clearing, Kitty pulled on Kip's hand, drawing him alongside her. "You can open your eyes now."

A small house of white clapboard and mellow brick, the miniature of Montclair, stood before them, enveloped in sunlight. Dark blue shutters framed the eight-paned windows on either side of the fan-lighted door. A flagstone walk, bordered with late-blooming marigolds and purple asters, led up to the pocket-sized porch, and russet-red Virginia creeper climbed up the chimney.

"So this is your little secret?"

"Well, maybe not a secret ... but almost forgotten."

"Eden Cottage."

"Yes." Kitty let out the breath she had been holding as she waited for Kip's reaction. "The traditional honeymoon house for Montrose brides—" She paused. "Kip, I want to live here. I mean, I want *us* to live here."

Kip stepped forward to look around. "Kitty, the place has been closed up for years. It's probably musty, full of mildew and mice."

She suppressed a little shudder. "But surely it can be cleaned up, painted, restored—"

Kip walked up on the porch, gripped one of the posts, peeled off a strip of paint, and shook his head, frowning.

"Oh, look, Kip!" Kitty pointed to the latticed arbor at the side of the house. Two built-in benches inside were shadowed by tangled vines, the leaves shimmering in jewel-like colors in the autumn sunshine. *What a perfect place for lovers to sit, sharing an intimate moment,* she thought.

But Kip had disappeared around the back of the house.

"The roof's been ravaged by squirrels, and the eaves over the windows look like they've nested generations of birds—" he called back.

"But it all *can* be fixed, can't it, Kip?" She caught up with him at the back door.

He gave her a long, reflective look. "You *really* want to live here?"

"Oh, yes, Kip, I really do!"

He brushed off the dust he'd accumulated and gave her a wide grin. "Well, then, consider it done. I'll talk to Pa and see about getting a consultation with a builder. We'll put a crew to work just as soon as possible."

"Oh, Kip, I love you so!" Kitty said, throwing her arms around his neck.

In retrospect, the only thing to mar her perfect happiness was Kip's seeming lack of enthusiasm. She wished he'd been the one to discover the little house and proclaim it the ideal place to start their life together. Wished he'd thought of carrying on the family tradition of spending the honeymoon year here. But what did it matter? At least, he had agreed to her plan. And they *were* going to be married and live happily ever after at Eden Cottage!

A few weeks later, Kip and Kitty were sitting in the small parlor at Cameron Hall. A fire blazed in the hearth, casting a warm glow over the room.

"Here, milady—the keys to the kingdom." Kip reached into the pocket of his tweed jacket and brought out a key ring from which dangled three old-fashioned brass keys. He took Kitty's hand, turned it over, and placed the keys in her palm. "Eden Cottage—all yours to do whatever your heart desires."

From his vest, he withdrew a legal-looking document. "It's all here in black and white, giving you the authority to contract for roofing, painting, whatever needs to be done. The deed to the house and the three surrounding acres are all in your name."

"But it should be in *both* our names, shouldn't it?"

He shrugged. "This just makes it easier when you're overseeing the repairs and restoration. You'll be on the scene, ordering paint, selecting the colors . . . all that sort of thing." He made a sweeping gesture. "We can change it after we're married."

Kitty's fingers closed around the keys. "Talk about dreams coming true." She sighed happily. "Ever since I was a little girl, I've always thought of Eden Cottage as some enchanted place, a fairy-tale house nestled deep in the woods, like the dwarfs' house in *Snow White*."

Kip looked puzzled.

"Didn't you read fairy tales when you were a child?" Kitty gasped.

"Guess not. Did I miss something?"

Kitty laughed. "Oh, Kip, darling! Never mind. We'll make up for it . . . we'll make up for everything . . . after we're married!"

"Well, just remember, I'm six-two, hardly a dwarf," he teased. "Just in case you're thinking of making any major changes in the ceiling height, that is."

Getting the house ready by June presented more of a challenge than Kitty had anticipated. In the first place, Montrose had stood empty for years, abandoned since Avril Montrose was married for the second time to Logan Cameron, and moved to Bermuda. Besides that, the structural restoration that had to be done took longer than anyone had foreseen.

In addition, since Avril had taken most of the furnishings with her, the house had to be completely refurnished. Kitty spent hours researching eighteenth-century materials to be used for curtains, haunting antique stores, and attending auctions. She wanted everything to be authentic, for the interior of the cottage to be as much like it might have been when it was built.

When she tried to interest Kip in helping her choose from swatches of fabric or pore over books of historical furniture, he proved irritatingly indifferent. "I haven't a clue about this sort of thing, Kitty." He threw out his hands helplessly.

"But you're going to live there, too. It's going to be *our* house, Kip, not just *mine*."

"Whatever you decide will be fine with me," he said firmly and that was the end of it.

The restoration of the little cottage became Kitty's project.

41

Much as she might have wished it were different, Kip rarely came over to inspect the progress of the work. Instead, he continued his daily trips to the flying field. She tried not to be jealous of Kip's preoccupation with flying, of the time spent away from her that they could have spent together, but it was hard when she wanted to be with him every minute.

Kitty comforted herself with the memory of a past experience, one that had made a deep impression on her. As girls, she and Merry Montrose had enjoyed wandering around the old tombstones in the cemetery behind the Mayfield church, reading the quaint epitaphs from long ago. One had stayed with her through the years: "What I gave, I have; what I spent, I saved; what I kept, I lost."

At the time, Kitty had not quite understood its meaning. But now, applying that bit of philosophy to her present situation with Kip, it made good sense. If she objected to his flying, made it into some kind of contest, made him choose, she would lose him. Just as Merry had confided to her how *she* felt about Manny's going out no matter what the weather, how afraid she was that there would be some kind of accident, that he would never come back.

"Finally, I knew I had to get rid of the fear. It was crippling me, crippling our marriage. For generations, the men in Manny's family have been professional fishermen. I knew that when I married him. I can't let my feelings spoil all the rest of our life together."

Wise words from her friend, Kitty thought. She'd have to learn to accept Kip's flying, too.

chapter
5

"WHEN DO YOU WANT to announce your engagement?" Blythe asked her daughter one morning at breakfast.

"Oh, I don't know, Mama. What do you think?"

"We could make the announcement at our annual New Year's Eve party. Or would you prefer a separate affair?"

"I think Kip's giving me my ring at Christmas—"

"Well then—" At Kitty's hesitation, Blythe took matters into her own hands—"since we'll need several weeks to make arrangements, maybe Valentine's Day would be nice. Such a romantic time to have an engagement party, don't you think?"

"I'll talk it over with Kip, then let you know." Kitty got up from the table, came around and kissed her mother on the cheek. "Thanks, Mama, for wanting to do so much for us."

"I just want you to be happy, darling."

"Yes, I know. And I will be . . . I am—"

Blythe smiled. "Where are you off to?"

"Eden Cottage. The painters are coming today."

"Then have fun, dear."

From her place at the dining room table, Blythe had a clear view through the window. As she watched her daughter's slender figure walking down the driveway to take the woodland path, she thought of the little house in the woods.

Eden Cottage! What memories of her own that name evoked. It was there, during her disastrously unhappy marriage to Malcolm Montrose, that she and Rod had first recognized their feelings for each other. Although that love remained unspoken for many years, the cottage remained a special place.

The week before Christmas, Kip, at a loss to know what kind of present to give his stepmother, Phoebe Montrose, begged Kitty for help in selecting a gift. She was secretly pleased but teased him unmercifully, boasting that she'd had her presents bought and wrapped weeks ago.

He grinned sheepishly but had a ready excuse. "I hadn't the slightest notion what to get for her. Besides, you'd know how to please her better than I."

"Actually, Kip, I don't know her that well myself," Kitty replied doubtfully.

Of course, she remembered when the young Scotswoman had served as nanny the summer she and Cara spent in England as children. But Kitty had been away at college when Kip's widowed father had encountered Phoebe McPherson again in Scotland, had fallen in love with her and brought her home as a bride to Montclair. At first, the Montroses traveled a great deal. But now Phoebe was the mother of a toddler, living a very different life from Kitty's.

Kip suggested the city would have a bigger, better selection to offer than the Mayfield stores, so they left early one overcast morning to drive up to Richmond.

Leaving Kip's car in the parking garage of the fashionable hotel where they planned to have lunch later, they set out to shop. It was quite cold, and the wind blew in gusts, sending flurries of snow in a swirling dance about their feet as they walked down the streets, gazing into the brightly decorated shop windows.

There was a bewildering variety from which to choose. By the time they had explored the third department store, Kip was ready to call it quits.

"We've been looking for hours," he complained. "Besides, I'm hungry. Let's go have lunch."

"But, Kip. We've barely started. Don't you have any ideas at all? Linens, china, crystal?" Kitty's voice trailed away. Montclair was already beautifully decorated, with many heirlooms passed down from previous generations of Montrose matrons. "What about something personal then . . . a silk scarf, a beaded bag—" Again she hesitated.

Kip's eyes brightened. "How about a piece of jewelry?" Once again in control, he took Kitty by the arm and propelled her down the street toward Simmons & Sons, a store on the next corner whose sign discreetly offered "Fine Gems, Estate Jewelry, Antique Reproductions."

Inside, the decor was understated elegance. Thick carpeting silenced their booted steps, and subtle lighting gave the place an atmosphere of hushed grandeur. The glass showcases were lined with mauve velvet with only a few selected pieces tastefully displayed.

A balding gentleman, splendid in a frock coat and striped trousers, a pair of pince-nez glasses perched on the end of a high-bridged nose, approached them.

"Good afternoon, may I be of assistance?" he asked in such a funereal tone that Kitty dared not glance at Kip for fear of giggling.

But Kip seemed equal to the occasion. To Kitty's surprise, especially in light of his initial uncertainty about Phoebe's gift, he responded confidently. "Yes, indeed. We'd like to see some of the estate jewelry, or perhaps some of your antique reproductions."

Kitty quickly stifled her urge to laugh, intrigued by the beautiful pieces they were shown. The salesman knew his jewelry and proceeded to tell them the history of each piece he showed them. One, in particular, caught Kitty's attention—a spectacular, deep blue sapphire ring surrounded by tiny diamonds in a gold setting.

Seeing the spark of interest in her expression, the jeweler spoke in reverent tones. "This is copied from a museum original. It is a reproduction of the engagement ring given by our Confederate President, Jefferson Davis, to his second wife, Varina."

"Oh, it's exquisite. Truly the loveliest ring I've ever seen." Kitty spoke in a near whisper. As a lover of history, especially the War Between the States, in which Virginia had played a part, she was fascinated by the story behind the ring.

Kip, however, seemed preoccupied. He was looking at a case displaying some necklaces and had missed the jeweler's discussion of the beautiful ring and its historical significance.

"What do you think, Kitty? Pearls?" he asked, spotting a nice strand in the case.

Kitty shook her head regretfully. "Sorry, Kip. I know Phoebe has pearls. She was wearing a double strand at baby Fraser's christening."

Kip looked discouraged. "Well, come on, then. I know she loves to read. Let's go to a bookstore. Maybe I can find her a book about Scotland."

Just then the jeweler cleared his throat and said diffidently, "Pardon me, but may I make a suggestion? Is this person of Scottish heritage, perchance?"

"Why, yes—"

"Then perhaps this—" He brought out a finely crafted

silver pin on which was sculptured a thistle set with a clear, lavender amethyst stone.

"Oh, Kip, look," Kitty breathed. "This would be the perfect gift for her. It's the symbol of Scotland, and I'm sure Phoebe would love it."

Kip was instantly agreeable. He asked the salesman to wrap the pin as a Christmas gift, and they were on their way.

In the hotel dining room, they dined on chicken *à la king,* rolls, and chocolate cream pie. Afterward, strolling through the hotel's arcade of fine specialty shops, Kip completed his shopping with a handsome leather writing case for his father and a cuddly Teddy bear for his little half-brother.

Kip was elated. "Now I have everything on my list. See how easy shopping can be! No problem to wait 'til the last minute!"

Kitty sent him a withering look. "You're hopeless!"

"Ah, Kitty, don't think I'm ungrateful. I'd never have been able to do this without you. Now let's go home."

"Don't forget. We have to go back to the jeweler's and pick up Phoebe's pin," Kitty reminded him.

"I'll tell you what. Since that's several blocks from here, we'll drive there. Then you can stay warm while I run in and get it."

Driving home, Kitty patted Kip's arm. "Well, that wasn't so bad, was it? Isn't it a satisfying feeling to find gifts that will please the people you love?"

"I hope so," he replied noncommittally.

In Mayfield, as they drove by the small Colonial church in the center of town, Kitty suddenly remembered her promise to deliver greens for the holiday decorations. Blythe had overseen the packing of the boxes, and Kip had placed them in the trunk of the car before they left for Richmond. But Kitty had almost forgotten they were there.

Kip followed her into the church, carrying the boxes of fragrant spruce boughs and holly, bright with red berries.

The ladies of the Auxiliary were still hard at work but greeted Kitty happily, exclaiming that they could always use more greenery. The choir was in the stalls, practicing Christmas carols, and the raftered sanctuary resounded with their joyous music.

Kitty and Kip emerged a short time later into a lovely purple dusk. A light powdery snow had fallen during the day and, driving through Mayfield, Kitty enjoyed seeing the houses adorned for Christmas with wreaths on the doors and glimpses of newly trimmed trees, their lights twinkling through the windows.

"Mayfield looks just like a Christmas card, doesn't it?" Kitty sighed happily. "I do love this time of year!"

It was already dark when they pulled up in front of Cameron Hall. Lights shone out onto the snow in welcome. When Kitty started to get out, Kip caught her arm and held her back.

"Aren't you coming in?" she asked. "I'm sure Mama's expecting you for supper."

"Yes, of course. But first, I have something for you."

"A Christmas present? But, Kip, it's too early. We always wait at least until Christmas Eve to open our presents."

"This is different. Besides, I picked it up today and, frankly, I can't wait till Christmas Eve to give it to you! I want to see if you like it."

"Of course I'll like it, Kip. I'd like *anything* you picked out for me."

"Yes, but this is special." She watched as he drew a small package out of his overcoat pocket. "I didn't want to give it to you in front of the others."

She took the small gilt-wrapped box, suspecting from its size what it contained, almost afraid to open it.

"Go ahead," Kip urged softly. "Open it."

With hands that shook a little, she undid the bow and carefully removed the wrapping. Inside was a gray velvet case bearing the name of Simmons & Son, Jewelers.

"Oh, Kip!" she gasped, looking at him.

"Go on, Kitty."

She pressed the spring that flipped up the top and saw within, glittering from its white satin nest, a sparkling sapphire surrounded by tiny diamonds.

"Oh, no, Kip, you didn't! It's Varina's ring!"

He was smiling broadly, obviously proud of himself.

Tenderness for him rose up within her. "How did you know? I didn't think you were paying any attention when I admired it."

"Nobody could have missed seeing your eyes light up, Kitty. I wanted you to have it."

"But you didn't say a word—"

"I only decided when we were there. But I wanted it to be a surprise. When I went back to pick up Phoebe's gift, I had the jeweler wrap it up for you. You *do* like it, don't you? I hope it's all right—"

His handsome face mirrored his sudden uncertainty. At the moment he looked so vulnerable, so like a little boy eager to please that Kitty hugged him impulsively. "Oh, Kip, it couldn't be *more* right! Here, put it on my finger."

"If it doesn't fit, the jeweler said we can have it adjusted."

She held out her left hand, and he slipped it on her third finger. It went on easily.

"Well, now, I guess it's official," Kip said. "We're engaged."

"Thank you, darling Kip. I can't begin to tell you how much this means to me."

"I'm glad, Kitty. You deserve the best."

She leaned across the seat, felt his cold cheek against her own, turned her face up for his kiss. His lips were warm, smooth on hers, and Kitty felt her heart soar. The kiss ended abruptly.

"Here, you're shivering. It's freezing out here. We'd better go inside."

Kitty hadn't noticed. She could have remained in his arms forever, but Kip had already hopped out and was running around to open the door for her. With his arm around her shoulders, they ran up the steps and into the house.

Kitty did indeed love her ring, but more important was what the ring symbolized. Kip must love her very much to have taken such pains to please her. He cared about her interests, what she liked, more than she'd realized. Though it *was* silly, she longed to *hear* Kip *say* more often that he loved her, but she decided that, with the ring, he had certainly *shown* her.

chapter
6

ON THE MORNING of the engagement party, the sky was heavy with clouds. The wind blew fiercely, and by afternoon a cold rain was coming down. Kitty peered anxiously out her bedroom window. If the temperature dropped and the rain turned to sleet, the roads leading to Cameron Hall would ice over, perhaps hindering the arrival of guests traveling from any distance.

At five, Kitty took her bath and, when she emerged into her bedroom, she saw that a fire had been lighted in her fireplace and a tray of tea and little sandwiches brought up for her. But she was much too nervous to eat.

Huddling in front of the crackling fire, she sipped her tea and tried to warm herself. But the chill seemed to penetrate bone-deep, perhaps more from anticipation than from the cold. Still, it seemed impossible that tonight her parents would be formally announcing her engagement . . . to Kip Montrose, the man of all her girlhood dreams!

Kitty gazed at her ring for long moments, turning it this way and that, the stones catching the fire's glow and refracting its light, winking and gleaming. As she had written in a letter to Merry: "I never quite believed that prayers like mine would be answered. It had always seemed too selfish, somehow too much to ask God to let Kip love me. And yet, wonder of wonders, it is true, and we are to be married in June!"

For a fleeting moment, Kitty wished Cara were here to share this evening. Then, quick to follow was a small, nagging admission that somehow her twin's presence might steal some of the shine from the occasion. This was *her* night, her moment. Immediately, she rebuked the unworthy thought. Still, she couldn't help recalling that once, not too long ago, Kip had thought himself in love with Cara.

At seven, Kitty took her dress out of its protective muslin cover. The rosy-gold satin shimmered in the firelight, igniting the tiny beads and crystals sprinkled over its tulle overskirt. It was the most beautiful gown Kitty had ever owned, even more stunning than she remembered it at her last fitting.

She was putting the tortoise shell combs in her upswept hair when a light tap came at the door, followed by her mother's voice. "Ready, dear?"

"Yes, come in, Mama." Kitty turned from the mirror as Blythe entered the room.

"How lovely you look! Kip will be dazzled."

As mother and daughter went down the stairs together, Kitty caught a glimpse of the transformation Blythe had created. Cameron Hall was a living Valentine! Bouquets of red and white roses in crystal vases had been placed under the mirrors on the marble-top tables in both parlors. The fireplace mantels and windows were festooned with red and white satin ribbons and bows, centered with lace-trimmed hearts and small gilt cupids. In the dining room, where later in the evening a buffet supper would be served, crystal candelabra held tall, twisted candles, and an elaborate floral arrangement graced the long table.

On the sideboard stood a three-tiered cake, decorated lavishly with swirls and pastry flowers on which Kip and

Kitty's names and the date, Valentine's Day, 1916, had been scrolled in sugared letters. At either end stood silver ice buckets cooling vintage champagne, awaiting the moment when the no-longer-secret announcement would be made.

Kip was standing at the foot of the stairs, talking with her father. His back was to her, and it was only when Rod's face lighted up at the sight of his daughter, that Kip turned.

He didn't speak but held out his hands, the gesture and the expression on his face speaking volumes. They had only a moment to smile at each other before Kip's father and Phoebe arrived.

"May I give my future daughter-in-law a kiss and welcome her into the Montrose family?" Jonathan asked as he and Phoebe greeted the honorees.

"Certainly." Kitty couldn't help thinking that in thirty years or so, Kip might look much like his handsome father, dark hair silvering at the temples, laugh wrinkles around his eyes.

Phoebe looked charming in an iridescent gray taffeta gown, and Kitty noticed that she was wearing the silver thistle pin on her shoulder.

"I love it," Phoebe confided as she greeted Kitty, then leaning forward, she whispered, "I'm sure you had a hand in selecting it, so thank you. It prompted Jonathan to give me these." She touched the delicate amethyst pendants swinging from her ears. "My Valentine gift from him."

"They're lovely!" Kitty was sincere in her admiration but felt a twinge of regret that Kip had not given her anything to mark the day.

Her momentary disappointment was fleeting because a moment later, Kip held out his hand to her. "Care to dance?" And he led her into the drawing room where the floor had been waxed for dancing.

The small band had been given all Kitty's favorite songs to

play. As Kip held her in his arms, they began playing "They Wouldn't Believe Me." She had always loved the lyrics to that song and, as they moved together to the music, Kitty could not help humming along with the melody. In a way, being here with Kip for the announcement of their engagement had the quality of make-believe. Some of the unsettling nervousness she had experienced earlier seemed to drift away with the music, and she knew that nothing mattered but being with him.

"Oh, Kip, I'm so terribly happy."

He smiled down at her. "I'm glad. You're absolutely shining tonight."

"Where do you think we should go for our honeymoon?"

He seemed puzzled. "Go?"

"Yes, after the wedding. Have you thought where we should make reservations? We really ought to do it since so many places book ahead."

Kip frowned. "I thought that's what all the renovating of Eden Cottage was about ... for our honeymoon."

"*That's* where we're going to *live*, Kip. It will be our *home*. A honeymoon is different. That's when a couple gets away together, just the two of them, to get acquainted—"

"Acquainted?" Kip looked astonished. "Good grief, Kitty! We've known each other all our lives!"

Kitty laughed. "I know that. But we have to learn to know each other ... as husband and wife—"

Kip shrugged. "Well, sure, but I don't see exactly why we have to go off somewhere. Everything and everyone we know and enjoy are right here."

Kitty looked startled for minute. "Maybe I'm being selfish, but I just thought we'd go somewhere without a flying field nearby!"

Kip threw back his head and laughed. "Ouch! I guess I deserved that. But I had no idea you were so devious."

"That's it exactly! There's a lot we don't know about each other. That's what a honeymoon is for . . . to get to know *everything* about each other."

"Oh, all right, I get it. So where would you like to go? The mountains or the seashore?"

Kitty was on the verge of answering when Rod tapped Kip on the shoulder. "May I dance with my beautiful daughter?"

Kip handed Kitty to her father, and for the remainder of the evening, the subject did not come up again.

The week after the engagement party, Kip suggested that the two of them go out for a quiet dinner. With several parties having already been hosted for the newly engaged couple, the two had been surrounded by people ever since the announcement of their forthcoming marriage, and Kitty welcomed the chance to spend some time alone with him.

He had chosen a new restaurant with a provocatively intimate atmosphere. Alcoved banquets upholstered in smooth, supple leather circled the room. Small peach-colored lamps shaded the tables, and in the corner a trio was playing soft music, creating exactly the right mood for a romantic evening. Kitty looked at Kip and smiled. How clever of him to choose this place.

When they were seated, Kitty studied the menu, glancing up occasionally to steal a surreptitious look at Kip's handsome face. She had never been so happy.

Kip ordered for them—an extravagant meal, explaining to the waiter, "It's a special occasion." And Kitty could not help thinking, *It's always a special occasion when I'm with Kip.*

They watched the waiter collect the menus with a flourish.

Then, with a stiff little bow, he left them to their conversation.

Kip leaned his arms on the table and cocked his head, giving Kitty a slow smile. "I have something to tell you . . . but I didn't want to spoil our evening."

"How could you possibly spoil it?" Caught up in the euphoria of the moment, Kitty was oblivious to any hint of trouble in Kip's words.

"I mean . . . we're supposed to be celebrating—" He seemed tentative, then added in a rush—"but you know how I feel about flying. You're the *only* one who does understand what flying means to me."

Kitty felt a small stab of disappointment. She hoped they were not going to talk about flying. Not tonight.

But he couldn't read her thoughts, and she was careful not to reveal her discomfort, so he went on. "Have you ever heard of the Lafayette Flying Corps?" The excitement in his voice was unmistakable.

She searched her memory. "Ye—es. I think I've read something about it in the newspapers."

"Well, then, you know that it's a single squadron composed of fifteen men. The Corps that was built up from this unit is a larger organization. A hundred or more Americans enlisted in the Foreign Legion for the duration of the war, then transferred to the French Flying Corps and are serving as part of the French army at the front."

"What has all this to do with you?" she asked, her heart already beginning to flutter with apprehension.

"Well, it's a fairly simple matter to join. Especially for someone who's already certified . . . I mean, someone who's been flying as much as I have."

Afterward Kitty told herself that she knew it was coming, knew what Kip was going to say even before he told her. She should have been prepared, but as she was to learn later, one is never prepared for some of the most important events in life.

Watching her closely, Kip took advantage of the pause. "Well . . . I've signed up with the Lafayette Escadrille—the outfit of American volunteers who'll be flying reconnaissance for the French Army."

Kitty's hand froze, holding her water glass halfway to her mouth, the ice tinkling against the crystal. She tried to respond but found her tongue frozen, too.

When she could speak, she asked the inevitable question, "When?"

"No more than three weeks at the most," Kip said, apparently relieved to have the news out at last. "All you need is a passport, which, of course, I have. Then fill out an application . . . Well, it's really quite simple, I'm told. While all the paperwork is being approved, you get your doctor to declare you fit . . . and that's all there is to it. Next thing you know, you're in France!"

"France?" Her stomach lurched, all desire for food vanishing.

"Yes, just imagine, Kitty! I won't be here champing at the bit on the sidelines of what's going on in the world. I'll be *part* of it. There aren't that many experienced aviators, so I've learned. I mean, the French are way ahead of us, and unfortunately, so are the Germans. But we'll soon catch up, give them a run for their money." His words were spilling out fast as his enthusiasm mounted. "It's a dream of an opportunity. How many people on this earth ever get to realize their dreams?"

Not I, Kitty thought dismally. Nor did it seem likely that her dreams would be realized any time soon. And what about the dreams they shared—marriage, home, family? Had he already forgotten?

Then, as if suddenly aware of what this decision would mean to her, to *them,* Kip looked anxious. "You see why I *must* go, don't you, Kitty?"

A hundred reasons why he shouldn't raced through her mind while Kip searched her eyes, begging her to reassure him, to let him go freely. But everything within her resisted. Now, when the happiness she longed for was just within her grasp, it was being snatched from her. Then a sobering thought broke on her consciousness. What if she did not give Kip her blessing? Wouldn't he go anyway? Either way, he would be lost to her.

"You do understand, don't you, Kitty?"

No! She didn't understand! She couldn't! *What about us, our wedding, Eden Cottage, all our plans?* She bit back all the arguments on the tip of her tongue.

Instead, she batted her eyelashes, mimicking one of those cupie-doll moving picture starlets. "I suppose you'll wear a blue uniform with a red-lined cape and visored hat, and look positively dashing."

Kip laughed. "You *are* marvelous, Kitty! I knew I could count on you." He reached across the table and took both her hands in his. "Of course, this means we'll have to postpone the wedding. But I don't think it will be long. This war can't last forever."

The night before Kip was to leave, Kitty found it impossible to sleep. Twice she turned on the light to check the clock on her bedside table. Finally, she gave up, pulled on her robe, and slipped quietly downstairs and out to the kitchen to warm some milk, hoping that would help her feel drowsy.

Still, she was almost afraid to go to sleep, fearful of the

recurring nightmare—one from which she always awoke, shaking and perspiring. She could never remember the details, except that at the point when she was jolted awake, she had seen a plunging rocket of fire.

Even after she went back upstairs to bed, she tossed and turned, awaking at dawn, exhausted.

Kip had arranged to say his good-byes to his father and Phoebe at Montclair, then would come by Cameron Hall, where he would collect Kitty and have her drive him to the station. He would be leaving his runabout with her in his absence.

Beneath the surface seriousness of his demeanor, Kitty sensed an underlying excitement. Here, at last, was the moment. Kip was on the brink of the highest adventure he could have imagined.

Kitty had already decided she would not spoil his image of her nor dampen his own high spirits by betraying the pain of this parting for her.

When they reached the Mayfield station, the train for Richmond and Washington, D.C., was already on the track. After parking the car, they walked onto the platform, then stood awkwardly, knowing they had only minutes to say all they had to say.

Kip put his hand under her chin and lifted her face so he could look into her eyes. "Well, this is it, darling. Now, I don't want you to worry."

She forced a bright smile. "Of course not!"

The conductor's call rang out, "All aboard!"

Kitty felt the edge of panic. She reached up and touched Kip's cheek. Her voice trembled as she pleaded softly, "Say it, please, Kip. Say you love me."

"Of course I love you, Kitty. I always have. I always will."

He kissed her. She closed her eyes, brimming with tears,

and clung to him, wondering how long it would be before she felt those strong arms around her again. Then she felt him pull back gently.

"Good-bye, Kitty. I'll write."

"Yes, I will, too."

The train whistle blew, and Kip looked over his shoulder. Kitty could tell that he was already thinking of the adventure ahead of him. "Gotta go."

He backed away a few steps, then turned and hurried toward his coach. The conductor had picked up the small yellow mounting stool and was preparing to board. Seeing Kip, he motioned him on. Kip broke into a loping run and swung up into the train. Leaning out, a wide grin on his face, he waved at her.

Kitty stood watching the train chug down the track, gradually gaining speed until it disappeared around the bend. The tears she had so valiantly checked, now spilled down her cheeks.

Overnight, it seemed, she had discovered what it really means to love someone. *Love means being willing to sacrifice one's own desires and goals for the beloved,* she thought, *even one's own needs.* She had let Kip go when everything in her cried out to hold him close. She had freed him to leave her and chase his dream. Even though she had always loved Kip, she had not realized before today how much love could hurt.

She walked back to the car in a daze, the echo of the train whistle as it crossed Mayfield bridge sounding hauntingly in her ears. Now she could release the tension of "keeping her chin up," of not giving in to her last-minute impulse to beg Kip not to go. He'd have hated it if she'd made a scene, but it had taken all her will not to.

Kitty got into the shiny green runabout, gripping the steering wheel, and leaned her forehead against it for a long moment. The rest of the day, the next week, month or who knew how long, stretched ahead of her in infinite emptiness. How could she bear it? What if the war lasted longer than anyone expected? And what if Kip didn't come back?

Finally she lifted her head, fumbled in her handbag for the car keys. She drew them out and held them, looking down at them in her open palm. The keys to Eden Cottage were attached to the same ring. Kitty felt her throat tighten. The keys to all her dreams, all she had hoped for, all she had wanted in life now seemed to exist in a dim and distant future.

What could she do? Wasn't there some way she could spend this waiting time usefully? Do something that would make Kip proud of her, something in the same cause he believed in so fervently? Something for poor Belgium, for France? Something that might even in a small way help bring the war to an end sooner?

But how? What? She must think, find a way. Kitty turned the key in the ignition, and the car pulsed to life. Suddenly, even as worn out as she was from tension and lack of sleep, Kitty's mind seemed clear. What was she good at? What came almost naturally to her? With remarkable clarity, Kitty began to remember her childhood—the parade of pets, the cats, the puppies, the birds that had fallen out of nests. All of these she had tenderly cared for and nursed to health—

In a war there was always a need for nurses. There were always the wounded, the injured and sick to care for. Kitty had read about Florence Nightingale, the valiant English woman called "the angel" of the Crimean War, who revolutionized the profession of nursing.

The more she thought about it, the more excited she became. Of course, she would have to take training. But what better way to use her time while Kip was away? And maybe

. . . just maybe, it would be possible to go to France. Surely, they would welcome American aid.

As she started down the road back to Cameron Hall, she could foresee only one obstacle—her parents. Would they object, try to stop her? Knowing her father's politics, how he deplored the idea of the States becoming embroiled in European battles, she felt a first wave of doubt.

He had certainly been outspoken enough, voicing his opinion of Kip's decision to fight for the French. "It's none of our business!" Rod had said. "It's not our war. The Germans and French have hated each other and fought among themselves for years. Let them settle their own affairs!" He was adamant. There had been no use arguing, no trying to convince him that for humanitarian reasons and in the name of Christian charity, America had an obligation to help.

Well, I'll cross that bridge when I come to it, Kitty told herself. First, there were other things to do, such as write for information about nurses' training.

Part II
Till We Meet Again

1916

Smile awhile, I'll bid you sad adieu.
When the clouds roll by, I'll come to you.
Until then, I'll pray each night for you . . .
Till we meet again—
     —from a popular song

chapter

7

On board the French steamer *Bonhomme*

Well, Kit, I'm really on my way. I could hardly believe it when I stood at the rail and saw the New York skyline drop away and knew I was actually en route to Bordeaux, from there on to Paris, and then to the secret air field "somewhere in France," where we'll be training.

I've met a great chap on board who, incidentally, is from California and on his way to join up with the Escadrille, too! What a bit of luck, right? His name is Vaughn Holmes, and he's about my age, although from an entirely different background. He's a real "cowboy." His family owns a ranch in the Central Valley, and he's practically grown up on a horse. At least, we have that in common, and, of course, our interest in flying. He's done a lot more reading and studying than I have about airplanes and the kind of equipment the French and Germans are using. I've already learned a great deal from him, although he's not yet actually flown. He'll get all his basic stuff from our French instructors, so I feel I have a leg up in this regard.

Vaughn also told me that the French airmen have been flying the Spad, a powerful one-seater that is the equivalent of the plane I checked out on in the States.

There are some French citizens on this ship, and at first they appeared to be somewhat aloof, even hostile, to the few of us

Americans traveling with them as fellow passengers. However, as soon as it was circulated via the ship's grapevine that Vaughn and I were on our way over to join up with the Flying Corps, their attitude changed dramatically. We are now looked upon as something of heroes! Sentiment seems to run high that it would be in America's best interest to come in and help defeat the Germans—

* * *

Paris, France

Dear Kit,

Know you would probably like more details about this place, the current fashions, art exhibits, etcetera, but I'm trying to concentrate on getting started with my training now that we're at last on French soil. Vaughn's father, I learned, has some friends in the diplomatic service here, and they took us out to see the sights. It was raining most of the time, and my sense of Paris at night is like a French Impressionist painting—vague and indistinct. They also invited us to dinner, and the French cuisine is everything it's cracked up to be! We're now waiting to get instructions on when, where to report—

* * *

Ecole Militaire D'Aviation, near Bourges

Well, Kitty, I'm here at last! And plenty ready to start flying. Even though I have my American certificate, I still have to go through the training steps here to qualify for a commission. I will be flying the neat little Blériot that I've had practice on in the States. It's a one-seater, so the pilot's in full control—start to finish—with no instructor with dual controls to take over. They feel that better pilots are produced with this machine.

Don't worry if you don't hear from me regularly from now on. Our daily routine is really full—every minute spent either studying or flying. My French is improving, but there is a whole new jargon emerging with the aviators.

We live in barracks—three big rooms, a hall dividing, shower at far end. There is a canteen on the field, a gathering place for the pilots, food strange but passable. I was relieved to find some very experienced men here, have been in the war since 1914, some Spaniards and Englishmen along with French. I'll be picking up a lot of tips from them. The conversation is an odd mix of languages, but all on the same subject—flying. We're all obsessed with it. But believe it or not, I'm doing a lot of listening!

Vaughn, it seems, is a born pilot. After only a few lessons, he's already got the hang of it. I think we'll move on to the next step together. It's a fine experience to be surrounded with men who have the same goal as I, to whom flying is more than some kind of hobby, as it is considered by most of the people we know, Kitty. Here it is serious business, and everyone is convinced it's the wave of the future and that, after the war, it will change the way the world thinks about transportation. Give my best to all your family.

As hungry as Kitty was for news from Kip, these were not the letters she had longed to receive from him. Even though she was interested in the new life he was living, Kitty yearned for one word of love, some hint that he missed her, regretted even a little bit postponing the life they had planned together.

To be fair, she realized that Kip was completely absorbed in the adventure, the thrill of it all. He wrote of the daily schedule, the camaraderie with the other men, the hours of study, the constant flying. She believed him when he said he was sometimes too tired to eat at night, just fell exhausted onto his cot to sleep only to be awakened at dawn to start the whole routine all over again. He never once mentioned the danger. But Kitty knew that it existed and that every time he went up, he risked injury or death.

Only once had he mentioned something about his life "before" in Virginia. He wrote that one of the fellows had an old gramophone, but only a few records that he played over and over, nearly driving the rest crazy. Kip said he had dreamed about being at a dance during that last Christmas he was home, hearing the music they'd danced to, only to find upon awakening that it was "that blasted, scratchy phonograph." Then he went on to say, "All the fellows complain about it. Sometimes, when it goes on too long, they throw boots, towels, and everything they can find in its direction to stop the music. But short of destroying it, which nobody has the heart to do, we put up with it."

Kitty read the short, scribbled notes again and again, trying to feel close to him. But Kip was living in a world Kitty knew nothing about. The longer he was gone, the more isolated she felt.

That made it equally hard for her to write letters to him. Everything in her daily routine seemed so dull, so tame compared to the life-and-death immediacy of the life Kip was living. America—safe, well-fed, going about its business as usual—was not an appropriate topic for a man living on the edge.

Oh, there was some effort to lend a hand, some activities planned to show interest and compassion for the cause. The church packed boxes of clothing for Belgian orphans and refugees, and the Red Cross held fund drives for medical supplies to be sent overseas. These facts she reported in her letters to Kip, but she kept to herself that life in Virginia went on as though men across the waters were not fighting and dying.

The thought she had had the day that Kip left kept returning to her in increasing intensity. Kitty decided to keep quiet about her plan for a while rather than risk an avalanche of negative arguments to dampen her own enthusiasm for the idea. In the meantime, she wrote to several nurses' training schools for information about qualifications and requirements for entry.

To become a certified nurse, all seemed to demand a commitment of three years of study and a year of actual hospital experience. Kitty realized that being a graduate of one of these schools was probably a requisite for joining the Army Nurse Corps.

A little disheartened, she put the brochures away in her desk drawer to give the idea more thought. She did see, however, that the Mayfield Red Cross Center was giving a six-week course in First Aid and Home Nursing and enrolled in it.

Then something unforeseen happened to replace Kitty's worries about Kip with a more immediate concern.

Late one winter afternoon, when she was trying to compose a letter to him, keeping it optimistic and cheerful, Lynette slipped into her bedroom.

"Kitty—" she began plaintively.

"Yes, honey," Kitty replied automatically, not looking up from her desk.

"Kitty," the little girl said again, coming to stand beside her.

"I'm busy now, darling. Why don't you go play?" Kitty suggested absently.

Lynette placed her small hand on Kitty's arm.

"Don't jiggle me, hon, I'm writing to Kip."

The little girl gave a deep sigh that merged with a racking cough.

"My stars! That sounds awful!" Kitty exclaimed, dropping her pen and turning to look at Lynette.

The child was flushed, her eyes glazed.

Kitty touched Lynette's cheek with the back of her hand. "Why, honey, you're on fire!" she declared. "I think you have a fever."

Lynette nodded solemnly. "I don't feel good."

"I guess not. We better take your temperature and get you into bed." Kitty stood and took Lynette by the hand. "Where did you get such a cough, I wonder?"

Lynette shook her head. "I don't know. I just did."

She settled the child in Cara's twin bed, then went to tell Blythe that she had moved Lynette into her bedroom so she could look after her in case she awoke during the night. Since Kitty had so recently passed her Red Cross home nursing course, she was glad for a chance to use her newly acquired skills.

She expertly applied a hot mustard plaster to ease the congestion in Lynette's chest, then brought her a drink of warm lemon-and-honey to sip.

"You'll be well in a day or two, honey," she assured Lynette as she tucked the bedclothes around her. The child was still shivering, however, and Kitty put a down comforter on top of the blankets.

Lynette stretched out a hot little hand. "Stay with me till I fall asleep, Kitty, please?"

"Of course I will." Kitty drew up a chair beside the bed. "Would you like me to read to you?"

Lynette moved her head slightly in an affirmative nod, and Kitty got out a favorite storybook from her own childhood and began to read: *The Secret Garden,* Chapter One, "When Mary Lennox was sent to Misselthwaite Manor to live with her uncle—"

When she had read five or six pages, Kitty looked over the top of the book and found Lynette's eyes closed. She put a marker in the page and laid the book aside. Leaning over the bed, she frowned. She didn't like the sound of Lynette's hoarse breathing.

During the night Kitty got up several times to hover over the sleeping child, troubled by her labored breathing, the periodic racking cough. Had they caught this cold in time to keep it from developing into bronchitis, or worse?

By morning, however, when the fever had not broken, Kitty suspected that the child was seriously ill. After consulting with Blythe, it was decided that Dr. Rankyn must be called.

"I'll stay with her until he comes. I'll try to get her to drink more liquids," Kitty told her mother and hurried back up the stairs.

Returning to the bedroom, Kitty was alarmed to find that Lynette had awakened but was rambling deliriously. When the doctor arrived and examined her, Kitty's worst fears were realized. Pneumonia!

That day Kitty took her post by Lynette's bedside, a post she barely left for the next two weeks except for brief periods of rest. It was an anxious fortnight for the entire household, particularly because of Lynette's "orphaned" position. With her mother dead, her father thousands of miles away, all the responsibility was upon Blythe, Rod, and Kitty as the child's condition worsened.

Each time the doctor came, he looked grave, making little comment other than "We'll have to wait and see—" Small comfort to the three adults who shared the nightly vigil in the long hours. Not only were they wrenched with anxiety but by the grim prospect of having to bear yet another family tragedy.

Gradually the prayers and skilled care pulled Lynette through. The crisis was reached and safely passed. The family could breathe again as Dr. Rankyn assured them of Lynette's full recovery.

To Kitty's surprise, in front of her parents, Dr. Rankyn praised her excellent sickroom care, then shocked her further by asking abruptly, "Have you ever considered nursing as a profession?"

This confirmation fueled Kitty's desire to pursue nurses' training just as soon as possible. Too much time had already elapsed since Kip left. With no end of the war in sight, no possibility of Kip's coming home anytime soon, if she wanted to see him, she would have to go to him . . .

chapter

8

IT WASN'T LONG after Lynette's recovery was well underway that Kitty learned that Kip had received his commission in the French Flying Corps. And the next communication she received from him was a letter written on the stationery of a Paris hotel.

September 1916

Vaughn and I are here on our first leave as full-fledged officers. His dad's friends are entertaining us royally. Already they've taken us out several times—to cafés, to restaurants for superb meals, to the Opera Comique, and to a play, in French, of all things! But I'm getting better at understanding the spoken language, at least. And there were French people in the company to translate what we didn't get, so it all worked out fine.

We've run into some other aviators in Paris on leave, and when we do, we have a regular gabfest. Some of these men are real "aces" with many downed German planes to their credit. Some of them are very superstitious and each have their eccentricities, mascots, and insignias. All are nonchalant about their exploits. But beyond their careless manner is a courage and gallantry that's rare.

We've learned that there is a code of honor that exists among pilots, Germans as well as French and English. For example, if a plane is shot down over enemy territory, as a courtesy, one of the opposing force's planes flies over the next day and drops a stone on a long, white ribbon with the name of the pilot and the number of his plane. Almost like the knights of old!

There is, of course, a great horror of being captured, as rumor has it that the German prisoner-of-war camps are terrible. Now, don't immediately begin to worry! There is little chance of that in my case. I'm becoming a better pilot all the time, full of confidence in myself and my trusty plane. Yours ever, Kip.

Don't worry! Easy enough for Kip to say, Kitty thought. He had no idea how many sleepless nights she'd spent, her imagination running wild. She was more determined than ever to get her training and go to him.

Then, before Kitty could consult her parents about her plan, a telegram arrived from Jeff Montrose. Her half-brother would be returning with Gareth, now twelve, from New Mexico, where they had been living almost since Faith had died as a result of the sinking of the *Titanic*.

The telegram announcing their imminent arrival sent Blythe into a flurry of activity. Avalon, Jeff's nearby island home, had been closed up for nearly three years and his unexpected announcement had given them little time to get it ready for occupancy again. Naturally, Kitty helped her mother in every way possible. This meant almost daily trips to Arbordale, overseeing the cleaning operations, stocking the kitchen and pantry, and hiring a staff.

After their arrival, Jeff and Gareth stayed at Cameron Hall for a week while Blythe fussed over them, trying to persuade her son to let Gareth live with them, at least during the week. He could attend Brookside Prep and get reacquainted with his little sister, from whom he had been separated since their mother's death.

Brother and sister were overjoyed to be together again. At

last Jeff was persuaded to follow Blythe's suggestion, but not before a compromise was reached. Jeff insisted that both children come to him at Avalon on weekends.

"I've got to get my family, my life together again, Mother," he said to Blythe, passing a hand wearily across his forehead. "Make a home for my children and start painting again."

He didn't mention Bryanne, and Kitty, listening, almost asked about the child. Then she thought better of it. Jeff had enough to deal with at the moment. Besides, since the sinking of the *Lusitania,* it was far too dangerous to think of crossing the Atlantic and bringing his other little daughter to Virginia. Bryanne would have to remain with Aunt Garnet at Birchfields, as safe a place as any in England these fearful days.

Life in Mayfield went on as if there were no war raging in Europe. The fall hunt and the social events surrounding this season were held as usual, with dinner dances on weekends at the country club.

In November, Kitty helped her mother, who was chairwoman of the Ladies Guild, plan the Thanksgiving tea to be given at Cameron Hall. The following Sunday at church came the announcement of a twice-weekly choir practice in preparation for the special Christmas services.

For Kitty, these holiday events to which she used to look forward with anticipation seemed hollow. Without Kip, there was no meaning in much of anything. Mixed with this unseasonal melancholy, Kitty had to admit some resentment. If he had not gone into the Lafayette Escadrille, they would have been married and spending their first Christmas in the cozy little house in the woods.

She had stopped going over there, unlocking the door and walking around inside. It made her too sad, too depressed, and since he had never taken much interest in fixing up the little house, Kip seemed even farther away. So she didn't go any more.

A week before Christmas, Kitty was busy wrapping presents when Blythe stuck her head in the bedroom door. "You have a visitor."

"Who is it?" she asked, but Blythe had disappeared, leaving Kitty mystified.

Puzzled, since she wasn't expecting anyone, Kitty hurried downstairs. To her surprise, she found Thaxton Collingwood in the drawing room.

"Thax!"

"Hello, Kitty. Surprised to see me?"

"Of course, but delighted, too! What are you doing here?"

"I've come to spend the holidays with my cousins, the Langleys." He grinned. "Hope I'll have a chance to see you while I'm here. That is, unless you're all booked up," he said cautiously. "There's a rumor you're engaged."

"Yes, that's right. To Kip Montrose. He's in France. He joined the Lafayette Escadrille, a branch of the French Flying Corps."

Thax looked relieved. "Well, then . . . if you don't think he'd mind, I'd like to take you to some of the parties . . . in particular, the Langleys' Christmas Eve shindig."

"I'd love that, Thax," she replied, genuinely pleased. Kip wouldn't mind. In fact, he'd probably be the first to suggest she keep busy so that she wouldn't miss him so much.

As it turned out, Thax Collingwood became her unexpected escort to all of the various Christmas parties given in Mayfield that season. Kitty appreciated his company, for it helped to keep her mind off how Kip might be spending his holidays.

She went to the parties, the dances held as usual. Those who saw her with Thax seemed puzzled, then a little embarrassed to ask her about Kip. In this part of Virginia, where society was sheltered from news of what was going on in the rest of the world, Kitty supposed they preferred to remain ignorant, feeling ashamed of them, of herself. If they did not have some direct connection, Belgium and France seemed too far away to be of much concern.

She kept up a good front, chatted, smiled, danced. No one would have guessed that beneath the smile, the bright conversation, she was harboring a pervasive feeling of sadness.

The poignant lyrics of a popular song summed up her feelings:

> *Smile awhile, I'll bid you sad adieu.*
> *When the clouds roll by, I'll come to you.*
> *Until then, I'll pray each night for you . . .*
> *Till we meet again.*

Dancing to the music, Kitty kept a smile fastened on her face, but her heart felt as if it were splintering into millions of pieces.

Christmas at Cameron Hall was festive as always. Since Blythe had first come here to live as Rod's wife, she had tried to carry out all the cherished traditions her beloved mother-in-law, Kate Cameron, had observed in her lifetime.

Preparations were started early. Decorations were lavish. Red bayberry candles were set in the sills of all the windows and kept burning throughout the twelve days of the season. Elaborate ribboned wreaths were hung on the double front doors. A blue and white Meissen bowl on the hall table held an arrangement of holly, magnolia leaves, pine cones, and fruit. A six-foot cedar tree filled the house with its spicy scent but was left untrimmed until Christmas Eve.

It helped to have Thax's cheerful presence in on all the family festivities. A few days after Christmas, he volunteered to drive Kitty into Williamsburg, where she had promised to take Lynette and Gareth for a special treat and to spend some of their Christmas gift money.

They took in the annual Christmas puppet show and had lunch at the inn. She was surprised to see that Thax was particularly good with the children. He had a wry sense of humor that kept them laughing uproariously.

On the way back to Mayfield, the children sitting in the back seat grew drowsy. And before they were fifteen minutes out of Williamsburg, Lynette—tired, happy, and with tummy full—was sound asleep.

In the front seat, Thax was talkative, keeping his voice low so as not to disturb her. "I admire Kip for what he's doing. In fact, I've thought of doing something like that myself. But my father's keen on my getting my law degree and coming into practice with him. I hate to let him down, only son and all that." He sighed heavily. "He keeps saying we should stay out of Europe's quarrels, that they'll never be settled anyhow."

When they arrived at Cameron Hall, Lynette had to be carried upstairs to bed.

Blythe insisted Thax stay for supper. "Gareth is staying overnight, and Jeff might join us, too," Blythe added hopefully. She went on to inform the cook of the extra guest for dinner, and Kitty and Thax went into the library, where a fire had just been lit.

Rod, who was sitting in his leather wing chair, stood to greet them, putting down his evening newspaper at their entrance. Inevitably, conversation turned to the recent screaming headlines.

"Those Huns—" He shook his head in disgust. "What they're doing is monstrous."

As horror stories of German atrocities had mounted, Rod's attitude had changed over the last year and a half. His outrage at the inhumanity shown helpless women and children had become a seething anger. He was now impatient that America should go to the aid of the embattled French and English and was now as indignant about President Wilson's policy of non-intervention as he had once been supportive.

"It's a bad situation," Thax agreed. "Do you think we'll get into it, sir?"

"With *our* President?" Rod put the question scornfully.

"But if America *does* come in . . . what then?"

"I think we'd get it over with. The British and French don't seem to know what they're doing."

Just then a boyish voice piped up. "My father says it's a sin to kill."

The adults turned in surprise to see Gareth warming his hands at the fireplace. They had not noticed when the little boy followed them into the library.

"It's the Germans that are doing most of the killing," growled Rod, reddening a little at his grandson's statement. "There's such a thing as defending yourself."

Just then Blythe entered the room and, with a quick sense of the mounting tension, spoke softly to her husband. "Please, darling, no war talk tonight. Shall we go into the dining room now, have supper, and perhaps afterward Kitty will play for us and we'll have some Christmas songs."

Thax left right after New Year's, and Kitty found she missed him. He had filled a void in her life, and now everything seemed bleak and empty again.

Later in the week, she received a much-battered Christmas package from Kip—a lovely silk scarf he had bought for her in Paris and a hand-painted card on which he had scribbled a message. He wrote only that he had a Christmas leave of three days and would be spending it with friends in a village near the airfield. The note was disappointingly brief, and Kip seemed very far away.

Seeing 1917 in had not been like the last New Year's festivities for Kitty. Dread for what the future held now replaced her hope and happiness. Kip's prediction about the war's being over quickly had failed to materialize, as headlines told of German advances, French retreats, British defeats. Now his letters were few and far between, never more than a few lines scribbled in haste.

Kitty decided to wait until things settled down to broach the subject of nurses' training with her parents. But again she was delayed, this time by a telegram from Cara, saying that she was coming for a visit.

chapter
9

ON A GRAY, windswept January afternoon, Kitty drove Kip's runabout to the Mayfield station to pick up her sister. She was eager to see Cara. These days there was never enough time to catch up, and there was so much to share.

Cara stepped off the train, wearing a beige bouclé wool suit, a bright scarf tied in a triangle over her shoulders, a brimmed felt hat cocked at a jaunty angle. She looked smart and elegant, though Kitty recognized the outfit as one she had worn while they were in college. Cara had always had panache, the ability to give anything she wore a flair. By comparison, Kitty, in her casual tweed skirt and sweater, felt almost dowdy. Certainly, her sister looked like anything but a parson's wife!

Rushing to embrace each other, their happy greeting collided with questions, answers.

"I can't believe you're really here!"

"How was Christmas?"

They were interrupted by the redcap bringing Cara's large suitcase and a big canvas bag, filled with gaily wrapped packages. Each grabbed one and, talking a mile a minute, walked down the wooden platform to the space where Kitty had parked the roadster.

Seeing it, Cara raised an eyebrow. "Kip's?"

"Yes, I'm its caretaker until he gets back." Kitty tried to keep her voice light as she lifted the trunk lid to shove Cara's things inside.

"Thought as much. It looks just like something he'd go for—" Cara said with a knowing glance as she got into the passenger seat.

Her sister's tone as much as her remark somehow put Kitty on the defensive. She started to respond to the unspoken criticism in Cara's comment but thought better of it. Anyway, she didn't want to start out her twin's visit with a quarrel, so she decided to ignore it.

Still, Kitty hadn't forgotten that Kip had once been in love with Cara, that since childhood they had been very close. As their old nurse, Lily, used to say, "Them two is lak peas in a pod," or as Jonathan, Kip's father, laughingly tagged them: "Janus—two sides of the same coin." Kitty felt a small stab of jealousy at the memory, but she quickly rebuked it. It was idiotic! What Kip and Cara had felt for each other was over and done with years ago. Cara was married to Owen, and Kip was in love with—

"How *is* Kip, anyhow?" Cara's question interrupted these thoughts as they started down the country road toward Cameron Hall.

"He's completed his fighter training and is flying regular patrols now, from what I can tell," Kitty replied, hoping she sounded cheerful and confident. She had to fight the daily fear of knowing Kip was in all sorts of unimaginable dangers.

"Isn't it just like him to do something as reckless as volunteer to fight in a war that isn't even America's?" demanded Cara. "Of course, I wasn't surprised to hear it. Neither was Owen. He says Kip was born out of his time. He should have been a knight in the Crusades or at King Arthur's Round Table, going out to look for dragons to slay!"

Kitty swallowed over the lump in her throat and changed the subject. "How long can you stay?"

"It depends—" Cara seemed hesitant. They were turning into the driveway of Cameron Hall now and up ahead they could see the house. "I'll tell you all about it later."

The evening was spent with their parents. Cara regaled them with an account of the Christmas program in which she had directed the Sunday school children. Kitty, Blythe, and Rod were all reduced to helpless laughter as Cara recounted some of the hilarious mishaps—the way the beard of one of the three kings, played by a ten-year-old boy, came unglued and hung rakishly by a single strand; how the papier-mâché wings of the angels flapped precariously when they climbed up on high benches to appear over the stable scene; how the shepherds stumbled onstage, tripping over their robes and dropping their staffs with a great clatter while the choir was singing "Silent Night."

"That must have been quite a performance," Rod declared, wiping his eyes when the hilarity had at last subsided.

"It was! In fact, one of the elderly ladies of the congregation came up to me afterward and told me it was the best Christmas pageant they'd ever had—" Cara rolled her eyes heavenward—"which only makes one imagine what the others were like!"

Later, when Kitty had Cara all to herself in the upstairs bedroom they had shared for so many years, she asked, "Are you really happy, Cara? Is being married to Owen what you thought it would be?"

"Oh, yes . . . more . . . better! Owen is so wonderful, Kitty. I can't tell you! He is goodness itself, such spiritual strength, such sweetness of character, such generosity. I don't deserve him, of course. But I've stopped worrying about that. I just thank God for him, and feel so blessed."

"It's just such a different life from the one we all imagined for you."

"I know. But I don't even worry about not living up to what's expected of me anymore. I found something in a marvelous book I've been reading in my morning devotions, and I've been trying to apply it: 'Begin to be now what you will be hereafter.' It's so simple, really. All you can do is try to do your best . . . just for that day."

They got into their kimonos and sat on their twin beds, facing each other.

"I have something to tell you, Kitty. I haven't said anything to Mama or Daddy yet—" Cara began.

Kitty, brushing her hair, halted. "What is it?"

"Owen's submitted his resignation to our church."

"What happened?" Kitty gasped, putting down her hairbrush.

"Nothing. I mean, no problems with the church board or elders or anything like that. It was his own decision—" Cara paused.

Kitty was stunned. "Why?"

"He thinks it's only a matter of time before this country is in the war. He's read about all the atrocities in Belgium and Alsace-Lorraine. He thinks America, as a Christian nation, cannot stand by and continue to be neutral in the face of all that's happening over there. He admires President Wilson but is convinced that honor will compel him to change his mind about our neutrality."

Kitty could only stare at her sister. It was so unlike the Cara of old to be talking so seriously.

"Owen doesn't want to go as a soldier. He's against the killing of course," Cara continued, "but he feels that when we do go in, there will be young men from all over the United States called up ... some of them mere boys from farms, small towns, tiny communities, suddenly thrust into a whole new life. They'll need guidance, someone to offer them some spiritual comfort, strength. So ... he's applied to become an army chaplain."

"When will he go? How soon?"

"He expects to hear very soon ... probably in a matter of weeks."

"Then what will *you* do? Will you come home?"

Cara shook her head. "No, if Owen is sent overseas, I want to go, too. So-o-o—" She paused, her head to one side, weighing the effect of her next words on Kitty—"I've volunteered to go as an ambulance driver for the Red Cross."

This announcement stunned Kitty. What could Cara be thinking?

Then she remembered that just a few years ago, their father had overcome his antipathy to automobiles and bought Scott a small motorcar so he could commute between Mayfield and Charlottesville, where he was a law student at the University. The twins had pestered him to teach them to drive. He was reluctant to do so because the roads around Mayfield were not yet converted to automobiles, and the going was rough over the ruts worn deep by carriage wheels. At last, however, he had given in.

"Don't ride the brake!" and "Engage the clutch *before* you shift gears!" were his commands that they practically heard in their sleep!

Kitty recalled her tendency to dissolve into giggles when this operation wasn't performed smoothly enough and the car leaped forward, bumping and bolting like a rodeo bull while the scraping gears screeched in protest. Cara, intent on proving her brother wrong for once, liked the feeling of power when she took the steering wheel and the sense of being in control when she was in the driver's seat.

Scott was surprised when both of them learned quickly. Finally, through their brother's less-than-patient instruction and her own dogged determination, Cara, especially, had become an excellent driver.

"Is there a good chance of your being sent overseas?" Kitty asked her now.

"A very good chance. In fact, probably *before* Owen goes. Ambulance drivers are in great demand, but they have to be trained in Scotland."

Kitty couldn't hide her conflicting emotions at this news. "Oh, Cara, I don't know what to say!"

"Please don't say *anything* until I have a chance to talk to Mama and Daddy, will you?"

"Of course not."

Cara stifled a yawn, turned back the covers, and slipped into her bed. "I'd better get some sleep. I promised Daddy I'd go riding with him in the morning. So you know how early I'll have to get up!"

Long after Cara's quiet, even breathing told Kitty that her twin was sound asleep, she lay staring into the darkness. The idea of taking nurses' training had never been far from her mind since the day Kip left. She had put it aside until after the holidays. But her experience during Lynette's illness had proved something. Certainly Dr. Rankyn had thought so. Now her resolve to carry through strengthened.

Besides, everyone she knew was now involved in the war in some way. Both Scott and Thax had joined R.O.T.C. and spent one weekend a month in military training at an army camp near the university campus. Kip, of course, was already in the thick of things. And now Owen and Cara. She was determined not to be the last to go.

Part III
Over There

England, 1916

This England ... this fortress built by Nature ...
... this precious stone set in a silver sea....
    —from Shakespeare's Richard II

The Hun is at the Gate! ...
What stands if Freedom fall?"
    —Rudyard Kipling

chapter
10

BECAUSE OF THE uncertainties of maritime travel and the security measures necessary in wartime, arrival and departures of ships were not made public, so no one was there to meet Kitty when her ship docked in Liverpool one typically foggy English morning.

After being checked through the big, drafty terminal, she took a cab to the railroad station to catch the train to London. Her father's sister, Garnet Devlin, had closed her London town house for the "duration" and was living now at her country place, Birchfields, which had been turned into a convalescent home for soldiers. Kitty planned to get in touch with her soon, but first she had to find a place to stay in the city and start the necessary procedures to gain a nursing position.

It was extremely cold in the small compartment. All the things yet to be done began to weigh upon her mind as she hunched her shoulders trying to keep warm. Until now she had been buoyed by the excitement and novelty of her adventure. Suddenly, all Kitty's dauntlessness, so carefully contrived for the benefit of her dubious family and friends, vanished, and in its place were loneliness and apprehension about the future.

It was already dark when the train pulled into London. The huge London station, crowded with uniformed soldiers, was a scene of frenzied activity. Tired and nervous, Kitty pushed through the doors leading out onto the street. After a long wait in the chill dampness, she was able to hail a taxi. Breathless with relief, she gave the driver the first name that came to mind, remembering only that it was a hotel where some of her relatives had stayed while in the city.

In spite of the lateness of the hour, no street lamps were lighted. They crawled in thick traffic through darkened streets.

"It's because of them narsty German Zepplins, miss," said her driver in an almost unintelligible Cockney. "Don't never know when they're comin'."

This information only added to Kitty's overstimulated nervous system, and she sat straight up on the edge of the seat until the cab came to a stop in front of the Savoy Hotel.

In spite of her heightened state, Kitty was physically exhausted from all the hours of travel. She found the soft bed and down quilt in her well-appointed room welcome and soon fell asleep.

The next thing she knew, she was being awakened by the entrance of a chambermaid bringing her tea and the morning paper. With this kind of service, she suspected that this hotel was much too expensive for a prolonged stay. She'd have to look up the small but respectable family-style hotel on Trafalgar Square a fellow passenger on the ship had suggested.

Surely, as soon as she let Volunteer Aides Department— VAD—headquarters know she was here, she'd be assigned to a French hospital. A matter of days perhaps. Or a week at the most. She wouldn't be here very long, but while she was here, she would enjoy her stay.

Looking through the paper, she was pleased and amused to see that Grace Comfort's column, "Inspirational Moments," was in its usual place. She remembered the huge surprise that had become a family secret when it was learned that the *real* Grace Comfort was not the wise old lady who dispensed daily encouragement to thousands of readers but a sophisticated middle-aged *man,* Victor Ridgeway, now married to her cousin, Lenora Bondurant!

Kitty read this day's piece with special interest: "Be strong and of good courage," wrote Victor, quoting the prophet Jeremiah. "I will never leave you nor forsake you." Just what she needed to hear. The word *comfort* meant "to give strength," she knew. Certainly that's what Victor did, day after day, week after week.

She had often heard her mother say that Victor Ridgeway was a very unpretentious person, dismissing his talent as "minor," minimizing the significance or influence of the column. But Lenora often wrote to them, testifying to the hundreds of letters he received from people whose lives he had touched.

As soon as she got dressed, Kitty decided to see London by day. She had not been here since 1914 when she had brought Lynette to visit her Grandmother Devlin and her little sister, Bryanne. But then Garnet had met them and taken them at once to her town house for one night. The next day she had whisked them away to her country estate for the rest of the summer. Since the only other time Kitty had been here was when she and Cara were quite young—the year of Queen Victoria's Jubilee—she remembered very little about the city.

Catching a double-decker bus, Kitty climbed to the top level. From that vantage point, she viewed the London spectacle with mixed emotions. London was colorful and amazing. A panorama of people thronged its streets. All sorts of costumes reflected the variety of life lived in this great city—the stalwart policemen called "bobbies" in blue uniforms and bell-shaped hats with chin straps; boys in their school uniforms, looking as if they might have stepped out of a Dickens novel; smartly dressed businessmen in bowlers, carrying the ubiquitous umbrellas and briefcases. There were dark-bearded men in turbans, probably from some East Indian regiment or another of Britain's far-flung empire, as well as Scots in kilts and puttees.

Yet, London seemed surprisingly peaceful for a country in wartime, Kitty thought. As they passed the park, she saw riders in fashionable habits cantering their horses along the bridle paths as if there were no war at all going on just across the Channel. She remembered reading about the gallant Belgians while she was still in Virginia, and how saddened and horrified she had been at their plight. It had moved her so deeply she had been anxious to come and do her part to help just as Kip was doing his. Here, however, it began to feel like a fantasy.

Later, when she re-entered the hotel lobby, Kitty noted that, at least on the surface, the dignified elegance seemed undisturbed. Uniformed bellmen were going about their duties with quiet efficiency. The luxuriously appointed lobby was filled with well-dressed people, among them a sprinkling of British Army officers in khaki and a few of the more flamboyantly uniformed French or Belgian military. From one of the dining rooms, music was playing, and waiters could be glimpsed carrying trays of delicious food.

Where was all the deprivation, the shortages Kitty had read about? It was as though the war in France was some far-distant episode, unrelated to daily life. It was all very confusing.

Kitty wrote to her Aunt Garnet, telling of her arrival, and

giving her address. She explained that she had registered both with the Red Cross and the English Volunteer Aides Department but had heard nothing from either one and would remain here until she did. She expected to hear any time now, but everything seemed to be taking so much longer than she had thought it would.

Every night before saying her prayers and trying to sleep, Kitty studied her French phrase book religiously. Sooner or later she would need to be fluent in the language. Yet most nights, her mind still churning, sleep evaded her.

Why hadn't she heard from someone at VAD headquarters? Especially when, almost daily, the newspapers reported the critical need for nurses.

Several days passed with still no word. Before she had sailed from America, Kitty had filled out an application, asking for an interview as soon as possible after her arrival. She had enclosed her certificate along with a letter from the Red Cross instructor who had taught the course at the Center in Mayfield, "highly recommending Katherine Maitland Cameron," stating that she had passed "all the required tests, was cooperative and meticulous in carrying out medical orders, was a skilled technician, as well as compassionate and competent."

By now, Kitty's funds were running low, so she decided to make the move to more economical quarters. Once settled in the smaller hotel, she continued her nerve-wracking waiting game.

Finally one day, frustrated with the delay, she acted on a suggestion made by her mother. Before Kitty left home, Blythe had written to Lydia Ainsley in London, telling her about her daughter's plans. She had given Kitty the Ainsleys' town address, extracting Kitty's promise to contact her English friend upon arrival. Suspecting that her mother's motive was to have someone "looking after" her, she had resisted at first, but now Kitty sent a belated note to Belvedere Square.

Almost by return post, Kitty received an invitation to tea.

Lydia welcomed her warmly. "How pretty you are and how grown up! My goodness, the last time I saw you, you were just a little girl!"

The charming woman took her upstairs to her sitting room at once. Seated before a glowing fire, Kitty looked about with pleasure. The room, with its rose-colored watered silk draperies, the elegant French furniture, the exquisite Chinese prints, was as softly feminine as her hostess.

"I had no idea you were already in London, dear. I only got your mother's letter two days ago. Of course, everything is so undependable these days, especially mail from America." Lydia Ainsley poured fragrant scented tea from a graceful silver pot into delicate Sevres cups. "If I had known, we certainly could have arranged to meet your ship."

Kitty took the cup and dainty napkin that Lydia handed her and selected a tiny sandwich from the plate she offered.

"That's very kind of you, Mrs. Ainsley, but we were not allowed to send cablegrams about our arrival. I suppose there are very strict restrictions about telling ship movements, with the submarine threats and all."

Lydia looked distressed. "Yes, everything about this war is so dreadful." Then she composed herself, the fine features resuming their usual serene expression. "How *is* your dear mother? I think of her so often. I still miss her. We were great friends, you know."

Kitty nodded and Lydia went on. "I felt for her so in her awful tragedy. And my darling Jeff. I am his godmother, you know. He was almost like my own son. To lose Faith when they were so happy, so ideally in love. Ah—" Again she struggled for composure. "I shall never forget the lovely luncheon Garnet gave before Faith and Davida left for Southampton to board the *Titanic*—" She sighed deeply. "Who could have known?"

Kitty, not knowing what to say to ease the awkward moment, bent her head over her cup and took a sip of tea.

"It certainly gives us pause to realize how brief our happiness, even our lives, can be. This war, horrible as it is, has made people consider what is really important. The things we used to do seem so inconsequential—driving out, paying calls, shopping— Why do we always have to learn the hard way?" She sighed again, then glancing at Kitty, she said, "Forgive me, dear. I didn't mean to be so gloomy. Tell me about yourself, your plans, and about your sister."

"Cara's in Scotland," Kitty told her. "She's taking a rigorous training course to qualify as an ambulance driver."

Lydia's shock was evident. "You modern young women amaze me! To think of that lovely girl, taking engines apart and changing motorcar tires."

"I'm hoping she'll come back to London before she's sent to France so we can have some time together." Kitty took one more of the delicious little sandwiches Lydia offered her. "Of course, I'm not sure how much longer I'll be here."

"Well, these things take time. Edward says everything is so much more complicated now."

Kitty held out her cup for a refill. "But the need for nurses is so great. At least that's what I thought when I left America. I thought they would be crying for volunteers." She sighed, realizing how weary she was of the waiting.

"Perhaps we could plan a little party. . . . Wouldn't that make a nice little distraction for you?"

"That's very kind of you, Mrs. Ainsley, but I feel sure it

won't be much longer now." Kitty wondered how the woman could possibly think of such things with a war going on!

At last, feeling restless and anxious to check for any messages at the hotel, Kitty dabbed at her mouth with a dainty napkin. "I really must be going. Thank you so much for the lovely tea."

Lydia looked troubled. "Oh, must you go? I hate to think of your being alone in the big city, my dear. We'd love to have you stay with us. We have plenty of room. Wouldn't that be pleasanter than that impersonal hotel?"

"How gracious of you, Mrs. Ainsley. But I'm fine, really, and I honestly expect to hear from the Red Cross or VAD headquarters any day now."

Lydia looked dubious. "Well, do keep in touch, won't you? As I said, these things always take longer than one imagines."

Unfortunately, Mrs. Ainsley's dire prediction proved true. It was another full week before Kitty received her long-awaited summons to an interview.

The starchy "sister," the matron at the headquarters of the Volunteer Aides Department to which she had applied, seemed singularly unimpressed by her favorable recommendations. She questioned Kittly closely, adding a somber note by saying, "Of course, you will have to undergo a period of training with us. Our methods are quite different from—" Here she glanced down at the portfolio of certificates and personal references, running her index finger down along the pages as if to check the name of the hospital nursing school where Kitty had trained—"from that of the States." Even that, Kitty thought, was said with a rather disdainful intonation.

Kitty bit back a retort. She was almost tempted to say something staunchly American but changed her mind. She was too anxious to put her nursing abilities to the supreme test to jeopardize her chances of being accepted. She longed to be where the action was or, to be truthful, where the chance of seeing Kip was more likely. So she kept quiet, not wanting to say or do anything that might negatively influence the matron's approval of her assignment to France.

Still, she waited, wondering if the war would be over before she was ever issued her orders or a sailing date.

Not expecting to be assigned to a hospital in England first, she was at first surprised and dismayed, then resigned when she received a notice to report to St. Albans Hospice.

chapter
11

Upon arrival at St. Albans, Kitty was given directions to the nurses' hostel across the courtyard from the hospital where she was to share quarters with another VAD. Entering the grimly austere red brick building, she was handed a key and told to go up the stairs to the second floor, Room 8B.

Kitty mounted the uncarpeted stairs, then walked down a long, gray linoleum-covered corridor and tapped once on the door. Since there was no answer, she used her key. The door opened into a narrow room with furnishings as sparse and as spartan as a monk's cell.

One side was already spoken for, as evidenced by a colorful hand-crocheted afghan folded neatly at the bottom of one of the iron cots and some photographs placed on the small chest of drawers. On one side of the closet hung a few garments other than the VAD uniform—a cape, sturdy boots on the floor, some boxes on the shelf above.

Kitty fought a fleeting wave of nostalgia, thinking of her pretty room at Cameron Hall and the luxurious one at the Savoy she had so recently vacated. But quickly she thrust aside such feelings. She was embarking on her great adventure, and this was part of it. With renewed excitement, she began to put her own things away. She was just hanging up her coat when the door burst open and a girl in a VAD uniform entered.

"Hello!" she greeted Kitty cheerfully, displaying deep dimples on either side of a deeply smiling mouth. "You must be my new roomie. I'm Imelda, Imelda Merchant. I'm glad you've come. It's been ever so dreary with no one to chat with since Gladys shipped out."

Almost at once Kitty knew she would like her roommate. Imelda was plump and rosy-cheeked with the kind of openness one could not help warming to, and an irrepressible sense of humor.

"You've met with 'Starchy,' I take it?" Imelda asked, flopping down on the bed opposite Kitty and starting to unlace her high, black shoes. She rolled her bright blue eyes. "She's a ticket, isn't she? Don't let her get you down. She rides all the new ones hard. She has it in for Americans. Thinks you jolly well should come in and help us out of this mess. Gave *me* a hard time, too. Coming from the North like I do, seems I don't have a proper accent, if you can feature that!" Imelda stuck out her feet and wiggled her toes. "Oooh, that feels good! Been on me feet for the last ten hours."

Bursting with questions about VAD life, Kitty asked them and listened to Imelda's frank answers.

"Well, you might as well know at the start that this place is run like a reformatory," Imelda told her with a wry face. "You've heard the expression: 'Cleanliness is next to godliness,' I'm sure, but Starchy truly lives by it. No self-respecting germ would be caught in St. Albans. Floors and walls are scrubbed down twice daily with disinfectant. The air fairly reeks with the stuff. And you can hardly get the smell off your hands, no matter how hard you try!" Imelda wrinkled her nose.

"Besides Matron, you've got to look out for the ward

nurses, called 'sisters,' and don't make the mistake of callin' them anything else, though I can't say why it's so important. It's not as though they were Lady Somebody or a duchess or something! They're tartars and keep you hopping. If you ever look like you've nothing to do, they'll make good and sure you do, and that will usually be the dirtiest job of the lot!"

Kitty's expression must have registered some alarm, for Imelda giggled and quickly reassured her. "Oh, don't worry, love, you'll do fine, I'm sure. Just keep reminding yourself it's not the end of the world."

Studying the family photographs Kitty had arranged on her small bureau, Imelda pointed to one of Blythe. "Is that your mum?"

"Yes, and that's my brother Scott. And this is my sister." She held up the snapshot of Cara in her ambulance driver's uniform.

"Sure, and she's the spittin' image of *you!*"

"We're twins."

"*No!*" Imelda put her hand to her breast in mock surprise, declaring comically, "I'd never have guessed!" Then she asked, "So she's over here, too?"

"Yes, in Scotland. She's taking her training there. I'm afraid she's going to get to France before I do."

"Well, St. Albans is the test," Imelda said, suddenly serious. "If you pass muster here under Starchy, you'll be in demand by the army doctors over there. They *know* she'd never send an unprepared nurse to a French field hospital."

Finally Imelda yawned, pulled the afghan around her shoulders, and curled up to get "a bit of shut-eye."

The days and weeks that followed proved Kitty's first impression of Imelda Merchant correct. Besides her obvious good-natured personality, her roommate also possessed other invaluable character traits—a generous spirit and an even temper—that made her a genuine friend.

Kitty's duties started the very next morning when she reported to her ward at six o'clock to begin a twelve-hour day.

She soon discovered the routine at St. Albans was more regimented than the Army. Everything was scheduled to the minute—doctors' rounds, bedmaking, patients' baths, meals, rubdowns. All the VADs worked under the eagle-eyed head sisters on each ward. Imelda had not exaggerated. There was never a spare moment in the long, arduous day, and all Kitty's training and skills were put to the test every hour she was on duty.

During the first two weeks, Kitty was so exhausted at the end of her shift that she could barely stumble up the steps to her room to collapse onto her bed. She was even too tired to get up for meals. But Imelda would shake her awake and force her up to walk to the dining hall.

"It's not worth it," Kitty would moan, thinking of the flat, tasteless food served to the staff.

But Imelda was ruthless. "You've got to eat, Kitty. Got to keep up your strength. If your resistance is low, you could get sick. Then you'd *never* get to France!"

This was usually all it took to get Kitty moving again. Then she would force down the unpalatable food, crawl back upstairs to bed again, wake the next morning to another day of relentless work.

Kitty had been at St. Albans for nearly a month when she was sent out for the first time on ambulance duty to the railroad station. Here they parked to wait for the incoming trainloads of wounded men. Nurses boarded first to evaluate the injuries. Most were suffering from shrapnel wounds. Accompanied by the VADs, who carried supplies of cotton, swabs, bandages, disinfectant, and iodine, they did some initial care. But mostly they tagged which men went where.

Those requiring surgery would be sent to the better-equipped hospitals staffed with army doctors and surgeons. Others went to private hospitals, while the less seriously wounded would go to the suburbs, where many of the large residences had been turned into convalescent homes.

It was Kitty's first experience in seeing the actual results of warfare, and she was sickened and shaken. She must have successfully covered her reaction, however, for on their way back to St. Albans at the end of the day, the sister she had assisted said tersely, "Well done, Cameron."

At St. Albans, off-duty hours were equally supervised, allotted, and monitored. No one was allowed to go anywhere or see anyone outside the post without official permission obtained directly from their ward nurse, the matron, or a doctor. VADs were expected to sign in and out, stating their destination and time of check-out and return, and everyone was required to be in by ten at night. Sometimes Kitty and Imelda managed to have the same time off and went to a cinema or to a teashop as a pleasant change from their routine.

One afternoon, after Kitty had been at St. Albans for six weeks, she was summoned by her ward nurse and informed that she had a visitor in the day room and told, "You may take a fifteen-minute break."

"But who—" Kitty started to ask, but Sister Clemmons had already turned away and was busy at her charts.

Who was the mystery caller? she wondered as she hurried out through the ward into the hall. She didn't know anyone in London except Lydia Ainsley. Mrs. Ainsley usually sent a written invitation rather than stopping by the hospital.

As Kitty pushed open the door into the visitors' lounge, she saw a slim woman in a dark blue uniform looking out one of the long windows.

At Kitty's entrance, the young woman whirled around and, seeing her, struck a dramatic pose. "Voilá! Behold, a licensed Red Cross ambulance driver!"

"Cara!" Kitty exclaimed, and the two rushed into each other's arms.

"Oh, Kitty, it's been ages since I saw you last!"

"When did you get here, and how long can you stay?"

"Not long, I'm afraid. I'm leaving day after tomorrow for France."

"*No!*"

"*Yes!* It's official. I have my papers." Cara nodded, holding her twin at arm's length. "But at least we have this evening. I don't have to be back at the hostel until ten. So see if you can get off and we can go out somewhere."

"I'm not sure I can—" Kitty hesitated. "They're awfully strict here."

"But surely *this* is an exception to their rules. Your twin leaving for the war zone? Try, Kitty."

"But you don't know our matron—"

"Oh, do go on. Don't be such a mouse. Every minute counts!"

On her way to the matron's office, Kitty ran into Imelda just getting off her shift. She told her where she was headed and why.

Imelda grabbed her arm. "Come on! I'll go with you to beard the lioness in her den. And don't worry, I'll take the rest of your shift. Now, don't argue," she said, steering her firmly along. "She can't turn you down. After all, it's her patriotic duty, since your sister's on her way to serve the country."

In a matter of minutes, it was settled. Then Kitty took Cara to meet Imelda, and they all went upstairs so Kitty could get her cape and the hat VADs wore outside.

Imelda couldn't get over their striking resemblance. "Did you ever play tricks? Try to fool your boyfriends?"

The twins exchanged a look.

"Not really. But we gave people enough trouble without doing it on purpose."

"Besides, I'm married." Cara held out her left hand to show Imelda her wedding band.

"And he never got the two of you mixed up? Before the wedding, I mean?"

"He's a minister. Has special discernment," replied Cara with pretended sanctimoniousness. Then she laughed gaily, and Imelda joined in a little sheepishly.

"Well, now that I think about it, for all you look so much alike, it's easy enough to tell the two of you apart. Kitty, here, is much—"

"Sweeter, nicer!" Cara filled in for her.

"I wasn't going to say that," protested Imelda. "Just . . . different."

"Cara's a terrible tease, Imelda," Kitty said, smiling affectionately at her sister. "Don't let her get to you."

"Have a good time, you two!" Imelda called after them as the twins linked arms and went out the door.

Soon they were seated in a busy pub near the hospital. Imelda had recommended the place as "quite a respectable spot for ladies dining alone." After ordering meat pies and a pot of tea, the sisters settled down to exchange reports on their new lives.

"Now, tell me all about Scotland and your training," prompted Kitty eagerly.

"Well, I didn't see much of the fabled land of poets and authors. We were billeted at a farm in the Highlands where they've never heard of central heating!" Cara gave a demonstrative shiver. "We were up before dawn, given a breakfast of strong tea and oatmeal porridge—believe me, I felt like Oliver Twist—only I *didn't* ask for 'more'!" She grabbed her spoon and gave a convincing performance of a small boy demanding his dinner.

"Then while it was still dark, we marched out into the cold to work on a bunch of ramshackle Ford trucks. We learned to strip engines, rebuild them, improvise repairs. All of that took days. At night, we had first-aid classes and practiced on each other, splinting broken bones and learning how to use different kinds of bandages. They even had us lifting sacks of potatoes and meal and putting them on stretchers that two women could carry, so that we could get used to lifting heavy bodies." She grimaced and gave another shiver.

"Then on to our French lessons. We studied a kind of phonetic, conversational French that should be enough for us to get by, so we were told—"

Just then the waiter came with their order, and the two turned their attention to the succulent meat pie, a tasty change from hospital fare. As they ate, Kitty gave Cara a sketchy account of her life at St. Albans.

She sighed. "I have no idea when I'll get my orders for France."

"From what I hear, they need all the help they can get over there—doctors, nurses, and drivers." Cara poured more tea, and for a few minutes they sipped it in silence.

"What news do you have from home?" Kitty asked at last. "It seems that mail takes forever to get here."

Cara shrugged. "Only that Scott got his commission as a first lieutenant in the reserves and drills on weekends. He agrees with Owen that it's only a matter of time before America comes in officially. Even Father has taken a different attitude. Oh, yes, and Jeff has finally consented to take a commission to do a poster for the war effort."

At this bit of news, Kitty's brows lifted. Their half-brother's pacifist leanings were well known.

"Oh, not for military recruiting purposes," Cara added quickly, "but a poster supporting War Orphans' Relief."

"And Owen?"

Cara's sparkling brown eyes clouded momentarily. "He's in New Jersey at a training base assigned to a company. We had a weekend together just before I got passage. I've only had one letter from him, but he promised to write every day, so the rest just haven't caught up with me yet. In that one letter, he said his men are the best. He's very dedicated to them and concerned about the bad press America's getting abroad because of President Wilson's stand." Cara shrugged.

The sisters' time together passed all too swiftly and, outside the pub, they hugged each other and said their good-byes.

"Be careful, and don't take any chances or do anything crazy," Kitty whispered over the lump in her throat.

"You, too, Twinny," Cara replied huskily, using the old term of endearment they resented others' using but sometimes used with each other.

"God bless!" they said simultaneously, then laughed a little.

Cara hailed a slow-moving cab back to the hostel from where she would leave with her unit the next morning. Kitty stood at the street corner, watching as it disappeared down the darkened street into the fog. She was overwhelmed with a sensation of abandonment. As had happened many times in their lives, her twin was leading the way into some new adventure while Kitty remained behind.

Walking the short distance back to St. Albans, Kitty wondered when she would see her twin sister again. Quite suddenly Kitty felt desperately homesick—for everyone at home, for the Virginia spring that would soon be blossoming, and for the little house in the woods where she had planned to live with Kip.

Kip. She missed him so much. Where was he tonight? Was he thinking of her, longing to be with her as she was with him? She hoped so, but she couldn't be sure.

chapter
12

Christmas Holiday

Heap on more wood! The wind is chill;
But let it whistle as it will.
We'll keep our Christmas merry still.
Sir Walter Scott
    —Sir Walter Scott

WITH THE SEVERE WINTER weather and shortages of fuel and materials for warm clothing, St. Albans was full of patients with respiratory illness. Nurses and VADs were kept quite busy. When one patient was discharged, another quickly replaced him. So when Kitty received a note from Aunt Garnet inviting her to spend the holidays at Birchfields, she did not have much hope of obtaining the time off.

To her surprise, Matron granted her a four-day leave.

"Mrs. Devlin has rendered invaluable support and service to our hospitals and outstanding effort since the war," she explained, "so go, and please give your aunt my regards."

Birchfields, several hours from London by train, had been turned into one of many convalescent homes for British officers, a halfway place where they could recuperate in comfort and seclusion. Most were ambulatory, although not yet well enough to be sent home or return to active duty.

The prospect of a few days away from the hospital sent Kitty's spirits soaring. She had not realized how much stress her daily routine of nursing had placed her under until the thought of being free of it, even for a short time, was exhilarating.

She packed her bag with a sense of anticipation, even putting in an evening dress she'd never had a chance to wear since coming to England, just on the chance there might be an opportunity to wear it.

Kitty was particularly looking forward to seeing Lynette's little sister, her small cousin Bryanne Montrose, who had remained with her grandmother at Birchfields after her mother, Garnet's daughter, Faith, was lost in the sinking of the *Titanic*.

Kitty traveled to the country by train. Upon alighting from her compartment onto the platform, she looked around with interest. The small village showed signs of change brought about by the war. The flowerbeds surrounding the brick station house were neglected. And a lone, elderly man, who under ordinary circumstances would have long been retired, was seeing to tickets as well as luggage. There were no buggies or motorcars waiting for passengers. Noticing that the handful of people who got off when she did were leaving on foot, Kitty set out to walk the mile and a half to the Devlins' manor house.

It was clear and cold, but her VAD cape and brisk pace kept her warm enough. Walking along the winding road brought back memories of the summer she had been here as a child— of going on picnics in a pony cart and of one special day when they'd gone to a village fair, accompanied by Jonathan

Montrose and Phoebe, then a governess. Kip hadn't been here that summer. Instead, his mother, Davida, had taken him and his sister, Meredith, to Cape Cod to visit their grandfather. Strange, but Birchfields was the one experience in her entire life that Kip had not shared.

The gates at the end of the drive were open when she arrived at the rambling stone and timbered Tudor mansion. The last time Kitty had been here, it had been summertime. The lawns and meadows had been a velvety green, the old-fashioned formal gardens abloom with primroses and pink and blue hydrangeas. Even now, although the grounds were winter-bare, there was a peaceful serenity here that made the war seem distant and unreal, in drastic contrast to the London she had just left.

There, the winter of 1916 seemed to go on forever. It had become the winter of the world in all its unremitting bleakness. The grim faces of its citizens spoke of the pervasive dread of the nightly threat of German Zeppelins, the wailing of warning signals, the whine of sirens tearing through the darkened streets, and most of all, the long line of ambulances moving toward Charing Cross Station to wait for the incoming trainloads of wounded.

Kitty thrust aside her gloomy thoughts. She had four wonderful free days ahead. It would be foolish to spoil them by dwelling on the harsh realities of her daily life as a nurse. Aunt Garnet had written, "I want this to be a joyous time for you, a few days away from the everyday grind." Kitty was determined that her visit would be just that.

Even so, when she entered the house and saw men on crutches and with canes, or with bandaged eyes, being led about by crisply uniformed nurses, she couldn't help thinking of the cruel irony of it all. That these luxurious surroundings should be ministering to the victims of the unspeakable horrors of war. Within walls where once gala balls and elaborate dinner parties had been given, where even a prince had been entertained, now men with broken bodies and shattered dreams were attempting to put their lives back together.

But maybe, by turning Birchfields into a convalescent home, Aunt Garnet was doing something invaluable for the men sent here to recuperate. By extending to them the gracious hospitality that prevailed here before the war, she was giving them a promise of hope.

While Kitty stood in what was known as the Great Hall, her aunt came rushing to meet her. "Oh, honey, it's so good to see you!"

"You, too, Auntie," Kitty said, thinking Garnet was as handsome and chic as ever, with hardly a wrinkle to show for her years.

"Ever since I heard you were in England, I've been longing to have you down. You're just what's needed around here. What a treat you'll be for these poor souls." She lowered her voice, still soft with a trace of her Virginia accent, as a man in a wheelchair was pushed across the hallway. "But," she went on, regarding Kitty with a frown, "you must get out of that ugly outfit at once!"

Kitty bristled automatically. She was prouder of her VAD uniform than anything she had ever worn in her entire life. But she overlooked her aunt's remark as Garnet rattled on.

"I do hope you've brought something feminine and pretty with you, dear. But, if not, never mind." She patted Kitty's arm. "You may have noticed I've put on a few pounds. It's the wartime diet, you know—too many potatoes! So I have some lovely Paris gowns I can no longer get into. You can take your pick and share some of your beauty with these poor boys who need cheering up." Taking Kitty's arm, she led her toward the stairs. "Come along, I'll show you to your room."

"Wait, Auntie. I'd like to see Bryanne. How is she?"

"Oh, she's fine. I'll take you out to see her in a while. Things have been rearranged, as you'll see. She's staying in the estate manager's house with her governess. Well, actually her nursemaid. There are simply no suitable young women available these days. They're all working for the government in some capacity or as volunteers like you and Cara."

"But why isn't she living here with you, Auntie?" Kitty was confused.

"Well, she is with me, Kitty. Just not in this house. I didn't think it wise for a young child to be subjected to so many distressing sights as she would if she were right here. Naturally, I see her several times a day . . . for tea in the afternoon, and, of course, at bedtime."

Kitty's face must have revealed some worry, because Garnet hastened to reassure her. "She's very well taken care of, Kitty. Maureen is a wonderful young woman, devoted to Bryanne. And the child adores her. You'll see for yourself when we go over there. First, let's get you settled."

There was never any use arguing with Aunt Garnet, so she went along submissively and was shown to the room, once Garnet's boudoir, adjoining her bedroom.

"It's tiny, but the bed is comfortable," her aunt told her. "I hope you don't mind."

"If you could see my room at the hospice, Auntie, you wouldn't ask!" Kitty laughed.

"I'll leave you then to unpack. I'll be back in a little while, and we'll go across the lawn and have tea with Bryanne," Garnet said as she left.

Later, when Kitty saw her little cousin, she had to agree she looked healthy, secure, and happy. Her features held the same promise of beauty as her sister Lynette, although their coloring was quite different. Bryanne's hair was a golden maple shade, her eyes a clear lovely blue. She had not seen Kitty since the summer of 1914 and was somewhat shy with her. Two years could seem like an eternity to a child. When Kitty began to tell her about her sister and brother in Virginia, however, the child's curiosity overcame her initial shyness.

"You do remember when I brought Lynette to see you, don't you, Brynnie?" Kitty prompted. "We had such fun together!"

Bryanne nodded solemnly. "She used to send me letters she printed herself and pictures she colored." She squinched up her little face questioningly. "But I haven't got one in a very long time."

"I know. Right now, the mail is very slow coming all the way from America, but I'm sure Lynette keeps writing to you. She would like to see you very much."

Over Bryanne's head, Garnet held up a warning hand and shook her head slightly. Didn't her aunt want her to talk to Bryanne about Lynette and Gareth, or her father? Kitty felt torn. She knew how much *her* mother grieved over her son Jeff's little family, how she regretted their separation. But they were Garnet's grandchildren as well as Blythe's, her beloved daughter Faith's children. Her feelings must be considered, too.

With the war going on, though, nothing could be done about reuniting them, so what was the use of aggravating this controversy between the two grandmothers? Sadly, Kitty did not pursue it further.

chapter
13

BY HER SECOND day at Birchfields, Kitty realized how tired she was. Her work schedule at St. Albans had been grueling, not only the physical labor but the added tension to prove herself. One of only a very few Americans on staff, she almost felt that the honor of her country was at stake. There, she had been too busy to think of anything but her duties, and at night, she was too bone-weary to do much but fall into bed.

Now there was time to rest and think. Of course, it was Kip who filled her thoughts. She had not heard from him in weeks and, although he had warned her of this possibility, she worried about him. If he had been injured . . . or worse . . . she would be informed. His family would have received official notification and would have told her.

But deep down, Kitty harbored an apprehension of some unknown danger. Not the recurrent nightmare from which she awoke panting and drenched with cold perspiration, having dreamed that Kip's plane had gone down in a spiraling arrow of flame. No, there was something else, something she could not name.

Before she left London, Kitty had written to him that she was going to spend Christmas with Aunt Garnet. She had even suggested he try to get leave and join them for a family celebration. But by the time she was ready to leave for Birchfields, there had been no letter from him.

Kitty had hoped that perhaps he might write her here. Each morning, she came downstairs in the anticipation that today's mail might bring some word from Kip. She tried to keep busy, volunteering for whatever needed to be done—reading to the men with eye injuries, writing letters home for others. Always a part of her was impatiently counting the minutes until the postman's truck from the village would come puttering up the long drive, and the mail would be sorted and placed on the polished hall table. But there was nothing from Kip.

Knowing that her Aunt Garnet was depending on her to help make Christmas a happy occasion for the men at Birchfields, realizing also that it might be the last some of them would ever have, Kitty tried to bury her own anxiety in activity. She plunged herself into all the holiday preparations, leaving no room for morbid thoughts.

Great armloads of greens from the nearby woods were brought in to be made into garlands to twine through the banisters of the staircase, decorate the fireplace mantels, and drape the balcony overlooking the entrance hall. The doors of the drawing room and music room were opened to form one large space, and a six-foot cedar tree was placed in the center.

A tree-trimming party was planned for Christmas Eve. Early in the evening, Aunt Garnet requested Kitty to play some Christmas carols while the men and staff gathered to participate in decorating the tree. The piano had been moved into an alcove in an adjoining room. While the trimming progressed amid lively chatter and laughter, Kitty seated herself and began to play.

Kitty played dreamily, memories of other Christmases at Cameron Hall filling her with tender nostalgia. In her mind's eye, she could see the snow softly falling on the sweeping lawns of home, frosting the meadows with white, going to church on Christmas morning at the small steepled church in Mayfield. As she played the old familiar carols, she was completely unaware of the lovely glow cast on her hair and face from dozens of candles.

This picture, however, was not lost on the Canadian officer who, drawn by the music, left his card game in an adjoining room and wandered over to listen. He stood in the archway and thought that he had never seen a more enchanting sight. Suddenly for him, Birchfields at Christmas had become a shining, magical place.

Pausing to turn the page of music, Kitty glanced over and saw the tall young man. His left arm was in a sling, and she did not recognize the insignia on his uniform tunic. Their gazes met. He smiled and she returned the smile.

As she went on playing, he walked across the room toward her and leaned into the curve of the piano, still smiling. He nodded and so did she, acknowledging him. His were the kind of good looks sometimes described as Irish—crisp, curling dark hair, high color, and strong, sharply defined features. Later surreptitious glances revealed that he also had the bluest eyes she had ever seen.

When she finished the piece, he leaned forward. "Oh, please don't stop. That is, unless you're tired. I could listen all night. You're quite good, you know."

"Thank you, but I think some people would like to dance. See the group over by the gramophone?"

He turned in the direction of her nod. "Then perhaps you'd do me the honor of dancing with me. I'm Richard Traherne."

"I'm Kitty Cameron. And, yes—" She tipped her head to one side, glancing at his sling quizzically—"if it won't be a problem for you. I take it your injury is not terribly serious."

"Not the kind that merits a medal for bravery." He chuckled. "I hope that doesn't disillusion you in case you thought you might be dancing with a hero." His blue eyes sparkled with good humor. "Actually, it was a motorcycle accident. I'm in Communications and was on my way with a dispatch when my wheel struck a shell hole and I somersaulted over the handle bars, tore some ligaments in my shoulder and leg, broke my wrist . . . . In fact—" He smiled down at her—"as it turns out, I'd say it was a *lucky* break! Otherwise, I'd be spending Christmas in the trenches rather than here at Birchfields!"

He came around to the side of the bench where she was sitting, and bowed slightly. "I hope you don't mind a one-armed partner. The wrist's almost healed. I don't really need the sling any more, but it wins me some sympathy." He laughed and Kitty joined in.

"Then I'd love to dance." She rose from the piano stool. "Shall we go see what records we have? I'm sure Aunt Garnet has brought in a supply of the latest tunes."

"Aunt Garnet?"

"Mrs. Devlin, the lady who owns Birchfields, is my aunt," Kitty explained as they strolled across the room to the record player where a group of soldiers and nurses was already gathered, looking through the stack of phonograph records.

At length a selection was made. The record was placed on the disk, the arm and needle set. Then the handle was cranked, and the music began. It was a piece Kitty remembered from summer dances at Mayfield Hunt Club.

In spite of the sling, Richard was an excellent dancer, leading her smoothly in the latest steps. She followed his strong lead easily, executing an elaborate turn, twirling around and back gracefully.

"I don't think you need any sympathy at all," Kitty teased.

"Vernon Castle better watch out!" She was referring to the male member of the popular ballroom-dancing couple, Vernon and Irene Castle.

They danced four straight dances. When it seemed that those in charge of the phonograph were having some dispute about the next record, Richard suggested they get some punch.

Finding two empty chairs in a corner, they sat down to talk.

"I'm curious," Richard began. "Obviously, you're an American. How do you happen to be here? Or do you make your home with your aunt?"

Kitty shook her head. "I'm a Red Cross nurse's aide with VAD. Right now, I'm attached to St. Albans Hospice in London, hoping to be sent to France eventually."

"I would never have guessed," Richard said quietly, his eyes traveling over her as if finding it hard to believe that this aristocratic-looking young woman, fashionably dressed in a blue velvet dress, with pearls in her ears and around her neck, could possibly be a hard-working hospital nurse.

Kitty blushed a little at the frank admiration in his gaze and quickly changed the subject. "What about you? How did you happen to join the Canadian Army?" By now, she had recognized Richard's distinctive maple-leaf insignia.

"Well, when I was a child, my father was in the diplomatic service and we lived in England for a few years. The summer after I finished college, a friend and I traveled through Europe. After that, I decided to take some courses at Oxford, and I was there when the war broke out. It didn't look as if the United States was coming in, so—" Richard gave a small shrug—"it just seemed the thing to do."

Just like Kip, she thought, then quickly amended the thought. Richard Traherne wasn't in the least like Kip.

"Nobody thought it would last this long," he went on.

"The talk was that the fighting would be over by Christmas, but I guess we didn't give Germany credit for being so tenacious." A grin broke through. "But let's not talk about the war. Not tonight. It's nearly Christmas, and 'tis the season to be jolly,' right?"

Taking her cue from his remark, Kitty groped for some lighter topic. However, it was Richard who turned the conversation by recounting some amusing incidents that took place while he was at Oxford.

"I didn't realize at the time how different our two countries really are until I lived among so many Brits. Wasn't it George Bernard Shaw who said, 'America and England are two countries divided by the same language'? Anyway, I was almost forced to buy a phrase dictionary so I wouldn't miss out on most student discussions!"

He gave a wry grin, Kitty laughed, then told him, "My brother went to Oxford, too."

"Oh? When was that?"

"Years ago. He's much older than my sister and me and our other brother, Scott. It would have been 1895 or '96. As a matter of fact, he didn't graduate. He dropped out to go to France and become an artist . . . much to our parents' dismay, I might add—" She paused. "Of course, now they are more than resigned. In fact, they're extremely proud of him. We all are."

"Why? Is he famous?"

"Well, I guess you could say that. He's won some awards. He's represented by the Waverly Galleries and has exhibited at the Royal Academy."

"I'm impressed. What's his name . . . I mean, besides Cameron, of course."

"Oh, it's not Cameron. He's my mother's son by her first

120

marriage. Actually, he's my half-brother. His name is Geoffrey Montrose."

Richard put down his punch cup and stared at Kitty. "Geoffrey Montrose is your half-brother?"

Kitty laughed at the look of incredulity on his face. "Yes. Really and truly, he is."

"Well, of *course* I know his work! That is, I've seen reproductions of his paintings in catalogues and art books. When I was at Oxford, I was at least exposed to painting and poetry. The whole place is haunted by poets and artists, you know. I wasn't a very dedicated student, I'm afraid, but I did absorb a great deal of ... I guess you'd say, 'culture.'"

Just then Kitty caught Aunt Garnet signaling her from the doorway. "I'm sorry, I have to go. My aunt seems to need me."

"My fault for monopolizing you. I assume you're supposed to circulate, spread your grace and beauty among us poor soldier boys—" Then, with a trace of irony in his tone, he added—"who will be returning so soon to the front."

Kitty reacted with spontaneous sympathy. "It must be dreadful for you."

"Sorry. I shouldn't have said that. I didn't mean to spoil one of the loveliest times I've had in months. You'd almost made me forget there *is* a war going on."

Kitty would have liked to say something to take that look out of Richard's eyes. She found him interesting and amusing and very likable, but she caught Aunt Garnet's impatient glance and said apologetically, "I really *must* go."

"Yes, of course. Maybe later? Maybe we could have another dance or two."

"I'd like that, Richard."

With that, Kitty hurried away to join some of the other

young women that Garnet had recruited to be hostesses for the party.

Her aunt had made every effort to make this year's holiday festivities as much as possible like those given in the old days before the war. In the dining room, small tables for six had been decorated with centerpieces of greens, holly, and candles. At each place were poppers, containing paper hats, to be snapped open. The hats would be worn during the evening's festivities. For every man, there was a little gift from the ladies of the local auxiliary.

As a special treat, Garnet had reinstated her own Cameron family tradition of serving "prophecy" cake for this special celebration. This year, so that each group of six would have its own cake, there were individual ones for each table. Inside each cake were baked six tiny symbolic items. A bell meant a wedding soon. A coin promised a financial windfall. There was a horseshoe for good luck, a thimble for a home blessing, and the most coveted of all, a wishbone, granting the finder *any* wish. Great fun ensued as everyone ate his piece of cake and found the symbol foretelling his fortune.

Kitty was busy serving during the meal and, since she was also expected to help clear away afterward, she did not see Richard again until much later in the evening.

He was waiting for her in the hallway by the door when she finally emerged. The party was officially over, the men who had attended in wheelchairs having been rolled back to their rooms and settled for the night. Only a few remained in the lounge and drawing room, chatting in small groups.

"I don't have a curfew," Richard told her. "Ambulatory patients are pretty much on their own. I hope you aren't too tired and we can pick up where we left off."

Nodding in agreement, Kitty led the way to one of the window-seat alcoves in what used to be Uncle Jeremy's study, and sat down. Someone had replenished the wood in the fireplace, and flames rose in brilliant blue peaks in the deep, stone hearth, reflecting on the brass fender guard. For a few moments they were content to bask in the warmth of the fire, relishing the companionable silence.

"I guess I'm being greedy. You're probably exhausted, but I hate to see this evening come to an end," Richard said at last. "It's been so . . . so special." The firelight on his face accentuated its planes, deepening the hollows of his cheeks and making his eyes appear opaque pools of blue. Slowly he turned toward Kitty. "It's helped keep the dark away . . . *dark* being that three days from now when I'll be back in France—"

Unintentionally, Kitty leaned toward him, her expression compassionate.

Richard spoke quietly. "After the hospital, coming here was such an unexpected boon that I'm still making the transition. I'd almost forgotten that there was anything else in the world besides the constant boom of guns, the whine and smash of explosions . . . the mud, the stench, the rats—" He shuddered involuntarily, then looked away from her. "Forgive me, Kitty, I didn't mean to—"

She covered his hand with both of hers. "Don't apologize, Richard. I understand . . . I do know, at least a *little* of what you've been through."

"Of course you do. I forget. It's just hard to imagine you in connection with . . . such dark and terrible things." His eyes took in the lustrous auburn hair swept up from the slender neck, a rhinestone butterfly nestled in its waves, the creamy skin where the folds of her velvet gown outlined the slope of her shoulders.

Her eyes regarded him with sympathetic understanding, and Richard burst out impulsively, "Meeting you tonight

123

seems like such a miracle. But in a way, it makes things worse. I find I'm dreading going back even more now—"

Kitty pressed the hand she was still holding.

Richard shook his head, then with an effort he smiled, and his voice took on an air of forced enthusiasm. "Tell me some more about your family, besides your famous half-brother, that is."

"Well, I've mentioned my brother Scott and a sister, Cara, who is now an ambulance driver in France. Actually, she's my twin."

Richard looked amazed. "*Two* like you? Impossible!"

The sudden solemn gong of the hall clock striking twelve startled them both.

"Midnight!" exclaimed Kitty, jumping to her feet. "It can't be!"

They looked around the room, now nearly empty. Only a few people remained talking and, in one corner, two officers playing chess.

"Have you plans for tomorrow?" Richard asked as he walked with her to the stairway.

"My aunt and I will be going to the village church, but you're welcome to come along, unless you'd prefer to attend the service here. I understand the vicar comes out on Sunday and plans to hold a special Christmas service for the men who can't get out to church."

"Oh, I'd much prefer to worship with you and your aunt, unless I'd be intruding—"

"Not at all," Kitty assured him. She turned to go up the steps. "Well, good night then."

"Wait." He put out his hand to halt her. "Since it's already morning, Merry Christmas, Kitty Cameron."

"Merry Christmas," she replied, looking into the eyes regarding her so steadily.

"Thank you for making this such a special Christmas Eve."
Kitty smiled, then turned and went slowly up the stairs, thinking that it had been a strange, yet a special one for her, too.

chapter
14

THE NEXT MORNING Garnet evidenced only mild surprise when Kitty told her that Richard Traherne would be accompanying them to the Christmas service.

"Oh, yes, that nice Canadian lieutenant."

Kitty excused her aunt's seeming indifference. Holidays must be especially hard for her since the double tragedy of losing both her beloved husband and daughter. Even with her dear little Bryanne's sunny presence to occupy and distract her, there was still a void lurking just beneath the surface.

The interior of the small church was dim and cold. Kitty slipped to her knees in the pew. Her first prayer was for Kip. Where was *he* this Sunday morning? Flying a dawn patrol in the gray skies over hostile territory? *Dear God, keep him safe!* She felt her prayers trite and unspecific and maybe ineffective. Could God really protect Kip from German guns and the skilled enemy pilots with their superior planes and greater experience? *Oh, dear Lord, give me faith to believe you will,* she prayed desperately.

But what about the prayers of German women for their sons and sweethearts? Whose prayers did God hear and answer?

Kitty shivered, and Garnet glanced at her anxiously. Just

then there was a stirring and shifting as the congregation stood for the entrance of the vicar, preceded by three small boys in red choir robes carrying lighted candles in tall brass holders.

Kitty tried to concentrate on the service but found that she was more aware of the man beside her. It was astonishing how, in such a short time, she felt she had come to know Richard Traherne. She sensed a quality in him beyond the superficial good looks and manners, the intelligence and charm. Yet even to admit her attraction to him might be dangerous. She was glad when the end of the service also put an end to her troubling thoughts.

That evening Aunt Garnet asked Kitty to entertain for the men once again since many at the Christmas party had requested an encore. This time Kitty selected some of the sheet music on hand.

With the first rippling chords, she began to sing along: "If you were the only girl in the world, and I were the only boy—" She had last sung this song at Montclair on Christmas Day two years ago . . . an age . . . another lifetime ago. She had been singing to Kip, although at the time he'd been too busy talking to Beau Chartyrs to notice. She remembered.

Now as the familiar words flowed, Kitty's eyes drifted toward the door. Richard had just entered and was standing in the shadows, leaning against the wall. The expression on his face was so transparent that she drew in her breath, and her fingers stumbled on the keys, missing a few notes.

She finished the piece, then stood and closed the lid of the piano. Moving to the window, she stared out onto the winter garden, blurred by the gathering darkness.

Soon she heard footsteps behind her, and Richard came up to stand beside her. "Guess what?" he said softly. "My cast comes off tomorrow. What's more, I've got the day off and the loan of a motorcar. Would you come with me to see the countryside?"

Heathercote Inn boasted the English tearoom of the tourist's dreams. While Richard helped her off with her jacket, Kitty looked around. From the small entryway, they stepped down into the main room. Heavy oak beams supported the low ceiling, and rough-textured walls further added a rustic flavor to the room. There were diamond-paned windows, and there was a cozy inglenook fireplace in which a welcoming fire was burning brightly.

As Richard helped her off with her jacket, she unwound her mohair scarf from around her head and neck.

A motherly looking woman with gray hair and rosy cheeks appeared through a door that Kitty presumed was the kitchen, carrying a loaded tray. "I'll be with you in a moment and show you to a table."

"Look, Kitty." Richard took her arm and led her over to a wooden plaque by the entrance. He pointed to the words carved on the surface, then filled in with paint:

TO OUR GUESTS

To all travelers, our door's open wide—
A haven for wanderers, a safe place to hide.
There's always a welcome any day of the year—
This is a haven of love, faith, and cheer.

"How charming," she murmured, looking up at him. Their eyes met and held for a moment, a moment that seemed somehow significant to Kitty but came and went so quickly that its possible meaning was lost.

"I can seat you now." A cheerful voice spoke behind them, and they turned to follow the hostess down two shallow steps and into the main part of the restaurant.

"What would you suggest?" Richard asked her. "You see, we're North Americans—"

At his remark, the woman lifted her eyebrows and beamed knowingly. "I took you to be Yanks." But she was smiling. "Perhaps, then, you might enjoy a typical English tea." ·

"Kitty?"

"Yes, that would be lovely."

When the woman left to get their tea, Kitty leaned across the table and spoke in a conspiratorial tone. "My Virginia ancestors would turn over in their graves if they'd heard her calling *me* a Yank!"

Richard whispered back, "I wasn't sure how she felt about Canadians, either!"

The ride in the open car had given them both an appetite, so they were ready for their meal when it was served. Kitty exclaimed appreciatively over everything—a squat pink and white teapot, matching cups and saucers, a linen cozy keeping the buttery currant scones warm, soft ginger cookies, and tiny cherry tarts. They devoured every morsel and, even before they had finished, their hostess was back with a fresh pot of tea.

They didn't lack for conversation. Their lively exchange of confidences about their childhood was liberally punctuated with laughter and sprinkled with anecdotes about their lives before the War.

They paused while Kitty poured tea, refilling their cups, and Richard fell silent. His expression was thoughtful, almost pensive.

"Penny for your thoughts," she teased. "Or maybe, since we're in England, I should say, 'sixpence'."

Richard sighed. "I'm afraid I'm going to wake up and find this was all a dream. I wish I could somehow stop the clock, make it all last."

"That's wishful thinking."

He reached into his vest pocket and brought out the small silver wishbone he'd found in his piece of prophecy cake, and dangled it between his thumb and forefinger. "Remember this? I think it means I get any wish I make."

Kitty took a sip of her tea, her eyes smiling at him over the rim of her cup. "Well, anyway, I hope it will be a pleasant memory, a pleasant interlude."

Reaching across the table, he took her hand. "Is that all this has meant to you, Kitty? Just an interlude?"

Kitty felt her face grow warm. But Richard was regarding her with such an imploring gaze that she could not look away.

"Maybe I shouldn't tell you, but I won't regret saying it, because it's true. I've ve fallen in love with you, Kitty—" He paused. "Is there the slightest possibility that you—"

She should have known this was coming . . . a lonely soldier facing who knew what kind of dangers. She should have told him from the first. "Richard—" She took a deep breath. "I'm so sorry . . . I'm engaged—"

He looked surprised, shocked. He picked up her left hand, examined the third finger. "But you're not wearing a ring. I looked right away to be sure. That first night, as a matter of fact, while you were playing the piano—"

Gently Kitty withdrew her hand. "When I knew I was coming to England to be a nurse, my mother suggested I put it in a safe deposit box. I couldn't wear it on duty, and it was too valuable to bring with me. But I *am* engaged, Richard. I should have mentioned it, I suppose. I just didn't think—"

The disappointment on Richard's face was so obvious that Kitty felt obliged to explain. "He's in France, an aviator with the Lafayette Escadrille—"

"And you love him?"

"Yes, of course. We've known each other since we were children."

"I might have known—" Richard's tone was disheartened. "It was foolish to hope. I suppose that's what most of us live on nowadays, though. Hope. The chance to grab a little happiness in all this madness."

He recovered quickly and they talked of other things. Then it was time to go.

Richard was silent as they drove back to Birchfields. Kitty huddled miserably in the passenger seat, feeling the cold wind in her face, and the cold around her heart. She was so sorry she had had to let him down, however gently.

In a way, she wished that Richard hadn't declared himself. Yet knowing that he loved her was strangely comforting. It assuaged some deep hurt in her, wounded by Kip's neglect.

Approaching Birchfields as darkness fell, the estate grounds held a stark kind of beauty. When they swung into the circle of the gravel driveway in front of the house, Richard parked the small car. They sat there, neither of them willing to speak nor move.

Finally, Richard leaned forward and cupped her face in his hands. Then he kissed her. She started to pull away, but the warmth of his lips, the surprising sweetness of his kiss, her unexpected response held her still.

"Kitty, Kitty," she heard him murmur before they went into the house, "why is the timing all wrong for us?"

The next morning, Kitty did not go down to breakfast. Instead, Garnet's maid Myrna brought up a tray with tea and cinnamon toast. Afterward, when Kitty put on her uniform, it felt unusually stiff after the days of soft knits, silk blouses, the satin-lined evening gown borrowed from her aunt.

Aunt Garnet came in to tell her that the chauffeur would

take her to the train station, as there were household supplies for him to pick up in the village.

"I hate to see you go, honey. You've been such a blessing. Your being here helped make the holidays bearable for me. And for others, too—" Garnet gave her a teasing look. "Especially that handsome Canadian officer. I do declare, I believe he's smitten."

"It's been wonderful, Aunt Garnet. Thank you for everything," Kitty said, giving her a hug.

"When this wretched war is over, I'm expecting you . . . and Cara, too . . . for a long stay."

Garnet bustled off with her handful of lists to start another busy day, and Kitty finished packing. Her time at Birchfields was already beginning to feel like a brief, magical respite. Now she had to go back to London, face the reality of her work, begin again the tedious wait for her orders to France.

She wondered where Richard was. Had he gone off somewhere? Last night he had told her he hated good-byes. There was something so hopeless in the way they had parted, a sad ending to their otherwise happy day.

Why did it have to be this way? Only hours before she had met Richard, Kitty had felt so very alone, thousands of miles from anyone she loved. Now, only a stone's throw away, perhaps, was a fine, honorable man who had offered her his whole heart, his love, his life.

She gathered up her cape, folded it over one arm, and picked up her overnight bag and started down the stairway. Halfway down the stairs, she halted. She saw him standing at the hall table, as if looking over the mail. At her footstep, he turned. Kitty knew, in spite of what had been said yesterday, that he was waiting for her.

It was the first time Richard had ever seen Kitty in uniform. The sight of her in her demure gray dress with its starched white collar startled him at first. Then he was aware of his immense longing to take her in his arms, hold her close, to breathe in the sweet fragrance of her hair.

He walked toward her slowly, both hands extended. She set her valise down and held out both her own.

"I don't want you to go," he said.

"I have to."

"But there's so much more I want to say—" he began. "I love you, Kitty. I can't let you go with so much unresolved between us."

"There's no use discussing it, Richard."

"But there may never be another chance," her reminded her gently. "I just want to know . . . *need* to know, Kitty. Before I go . . . do you love me?"

Kitty started to draw away her hands, but he held them tight. "You know I'm promised to someone else, Richard—"

"But . . . if you weren't . . . would you, could you love me?"

"That isn't a possibility, Richard. I never meant to let you think—"

"You didn't, Kitty. All I know is what I feel." He pulled her into his arms so she couldn't turn away. Looking into her eyes, he spoke urgently, "I love you, Kitty; I'd do anything in the world for you. Just give me some hope—"

Kitty closed her eyes to block out the pleading she saw in his, and shook her head. "I–I can't, Richard."

With a sigh, he released her. "Good-bye then, Kitty. Don't forget me, will you?"

"I'll never forget you, Richard—wouldn't want to."

"I don't know why, but I feel somehow, some way—" He paused, then smiled. "That's not fair, is it, Kitty? I do wish you happiness." He hesitated. "Kiss me good-bye?"

"Of course." She lifted her face to his.

His kiss was deeply tender. In it was all the longing of a

passionate heart. Kitty responded to its sweetness, its relinquishment.

When it ended, Richard said quietly, "I shall always love you, Kitty, as long as I live."

Kitty repressed a shudder. His words held such poignant potential. These days life was so tentative, so precarious. In another day or two, Richard was going back to France. Anything could happen.

In the train all the way back to London, Kitty wept softly. If there were no Kip . . . if there had *never* been Kip . . . she knew she could love Richard. She *did* love Richard, but she was not *in love* with him. There was a difference. Richard was charming, witty, intelligent, considerate—a gentleman in every sense of the word. Kip was . . . well . . . Kip. He was a part of her, of all she had ever been. And he would always be a part of her.

She looked down at her bare third finger on her left hand and thought of the other things she had left in the bank's safe deposit box along with the engagement ring—the keys and deed to Eden Cottage. She felt a chill as though someone had opened a window and let in a draught of icy air. Would she ever wear that ring again, or turn the key in the lock of the little house across the rustic bridge from Montclair?

Kitty had been back in the hospital in London less than a week when she received a letter marked "Somewhere in France." She scanned the unfamiliar handwriting and guessed before opening it that it was from Richard.

Inside, he had written:

> I told you that at Oxford I dabbled in painting and poetry, but I'll never be able to capture in words what last week meant to me, only to say it was like a dream, with timelessness and joy I've

never experienced before. Maybe it was a romantic illusion of what I imagine life could be with someone you love.

I enclose something I found recently and want to share with you, written by a Winifred Mary Letts:

> I saw the spires of Oxford
> As I was passing by;
> The grey spires of Oxford
> Against a pearl-grey sky.
> My heart was with the Oxford men
> Who went abroad to die.

I love you, Kitty Cameron.

Always, Richard Traherne

Kitty folded the letter and replaced it in its envelope. She hated the depression she sensed in Richard's words. She knew the awful waste of the young men whom the poet had written about. Didn't she see them every day? Some scarcely out of high school, others fresh from college campuses. But there was something else that disturbed her deeply, a kind of fatalism. Did Richard expect to die?

Suddenly Kitty was reminded of something that old Lily used to say when she'd received bad news, "Somthin' jest walked ober mah grave."

Kitty forced back the superstitious thought. She was being foolishly morbid. What did the Bible say about fear? She couldn't manage chapter and verse, but she knew there were many admonitions to trust God and not be afraid. Quickly she whispered a prayer of protection for Richard, for Kip and Scott and all the unnamed, unknown soldiers facing death. Then she went on duty with determined cheerfulness.

Only a few weeks later, Kitty received her orders to go to France.

Part IV
No Coward Soul

Somewhere in France

No coward soul is mine,
No trembler in the world's storm-troubled sphere:
I see Heaven's glories shine,
And faith shines equal, arming me from fear—
        —Emily Bronte

chapter
15

PALE WISPS of fog swirled about like shreds of gray cotton wool in the cold dark pre-dawn. Kitty shivered even under her nurse's cape, its warmth useless against the deep shudders she was powerless to control. She found herself praying, *Please, Lord, don't let anything happen to prevent my going to France!* No incidental error on her papers, no question about her eligibility, no last-minute hitch.

Her initial excitement at receiving her orders had been lost in the frenetic rush to complete all the necessary papers, send word of her transfer home, get her duty release from "Starchy," and pack. Now all that was left, after a hurried trip by train to this seaport town of embarkation, was a bad case of nerves.

At the train station her Red Cross certification and signed release from St. Albans had not been sufficient identification to offset a thorough search. She had been requested, though politely, to take off her shoes and empty her purse while another matron ran expert hands along the lining of her cape.

It was already past midnight. Heart in her throat, Kitty followed the straggling crowd of passengers and joined the line forming on the jetty under the shed.

"Ladies and gentlemen, please have your passports ready,"

139

instructed someone in a precise British voice. With a shaky hand, Kitty drew hers out of her handbag. An irrelevant fear gripped her that here, at this last minute, she might be turned back. Ridiculous, she told herself, glancing about at the others standing with her. Their faces looked ghostly in the yellow light, mirroring her own anxiety.

The line moved forward silently and slowly. Credentials were presented to the officer standing at the gangplank. Kitty tried to think of other, more pleasant thoughts. Then at last it was her turn. Her passport was studied for what seemed an inordinate amount of time, then the officer gave her a brisk nod and handed it back to her.

"All right, Miss," he said. "Next, please."

She moved quickly past him, up the gangplank. Then she was on deck. She moved over to the railing, leaned against it. Only then did Kitty realize that she had been holding her breath.

The wind off the Channel, moist with sea spray, was freezing. Gradually she felt the vibration of the engine starting up, the slow, rocking movement of the boat beneath her, sliding out from the dock, edging its way out from the harbor. As she gripped the rail, the boat plowed through the dark, dangerous waters of the Channel. She was on her way to France at last!

The wind grew bitingly cold, and Kitty left the deck, seeking the warmth of the lounge below. It was furnished only with plain wooden benches. Many of the other passengers had already taken refuge here.

Her fellow travelers were a mixed lot. About ten VADs from other training centers were also on their way to field hospitals. Kitty did not know any of the young women, merely recognized them from their uniforms identical to her own—the red-lined capes, the short-brimmed blue hats, the Red Cross insignia on the armband.

There were soldiers, too, some who looked heartbreakingly young, obviously on their first tour of duty. These men, laughing and joking among themselves, offered a sharp contrast to others with glazed eyes and hunched shoulders, perhaps returning to battle after leave.

It was a strange night, one that Kitty would always remember. Though some slept, her mind was roiled with many thoughts, interspersed with prayer. For some reason, a poem by Emily Bronte that she had learned in college came to her:

> No coward soul is mine,
> No trembler in the world's storm-troubled sphere:
> I see heaven's glories shine,
> And faith shines equal, arming me from fear—

Kitty hoped that she would be brave, hoped that she would not be found to have a "coward's soul" when she was faced with whatever lay ahead.

A gray dawn was breaking over a pewter sea when the boat nosed into the landing dock. Groggy and feeling rather queasy from hunger, Kitty followed the line of passengers trailing off the boat onto the dock.

After landing, the VADs were instructed to line up to have their papers checked by the French port authorities and once more by an officer from the medical corps. When their identities were established, verified by double-checking against a long list, they were given the name of the post to which they would be assigned. Kitty and four other young women were directed to a bus, which they boarded silently.

They acknowledged each other with stiff little nods and

nervous smiles, but no one spoke. Soon a sergeant swung on to the bus and got behind the wheel, announcing cheerfully, "Right-o, ladies, off we go," and with a great grinding of gears and the noisy scratchy sound of a rusty ignition, they started off.

It was getting lighter now. Kitty looked out the smeared window of the bus and saw the bleak, unfamiliar landscape.

From Dunkirk to the front, the road was lightly guarded. They passed village after village that appeared to be deserted. Beyond lay fields flanked by groves of poplar trees, and beside them a muddy canal slithered through the scene like a venomous serpent.

Even above the rattle of the vehicle, Kitty was aware of the distant sound of booming artillery. This was really it. She was in France. Not far away was the war zone. Her heart hammered in her throat, her palms under the woolen gloves grew clammy.

They must have driven for two hours. Kitty lost all track of time. Her head ached dully from lack of food, and every nerve in her body tingled with tension.

"Well, ladies," boomed the driver, "we're almost to our destination—formerly the Chateau Rougeret, now officially an evacuation 'ospital. This buildin' was once the home of the Rougeret family, who are, I'm told, quite the hoi-poloi, leastways until most of 'em lost their bloomin' 'eads in the Revolooshun!" He laughed heartily at his own joke.

Amused, Kitty could not help wondering if the sergeant had been a music-hall comedian before the war.

"Madame Rougeret still lives in part of the chateau," he went on, "although I don't know anyone who's actually seen her ladyship!" Once again, he stopped to enjoy his humor. "Maybe she's a 'eadless ghost! Who knows? Maybe the 'ouse is 'aunted!"

One of the other VADs sitting across the aisle from Kitty leaned toward her, winked, and asked in a stage whisper, "Do you suppose he's trying to cheer us up?"

Kitty shrugged and returned her mischievous smile.

The young woman thrust out a mittened hand. "I'm Dora Bradon."

"Kitty Cameron." She started to ask where she'd trained, but just then there was another announcement from their driver.

"For your information, ladies, the chateau is situated only ten miles behind the Allied lines, so don't worry, you'll have plenty of business, as they say."

At that moment the bus lurched, and everyone had to grab the back of the seat ahead to keep from sliding into the aisle and onto the floor.

As their vehicle chugged into a village which, from the look of it, had been the target of heavy bombardment, their driver began weaving crazily to avoid the deep shell holes blasted out of the street. In the field to one side, Kitty saw many little crosses, and the sight chilled her heart.

A little farther along, a platoon of men came marching alongside, their eyes fixed, faces grave and determined. A wagon loaded with artillery rumbled past them down the rutted road.

Protesting in backfires, the bus began a long uphill climb. Flanking them were dense woods. At the top, a turreted stone building was silhouetted against the overcast morning sky.

The bus braked at last to a groaning stop.

"Here we are, ladies—Chateau Rougeret!"

Stiff and shaky, Kitty emerged from the bus. She took a few steps and glanced around. On what must have once been terraced lawns and formal gardens stood several wooden buildings, looking as though they had been hastily erected.

"This way, ladies." The sergeant motioned them forward, and the little group followed him up some shallow stone steps and into a gloomy entrance hall.

Kitty's first impression was of impregnable cold. The great hall had the feeling of a fortress, untouched by sunlight for centuries.

"Wait here. I'll go fetch Matron." The sergeant left them and disappeared down a narrow vaulted hallway.

"Suppose that's the way to the dungeon?" quipped Dora Bradon, the young woman who had introduced herself to Kitty.

Unexpectedly, Kitty burst out laughing. Soon all four VADs had joined in, welcoming the input of some humor into this alien situation. With the laughter came a release of tension, followed by a round of introductions.

They had just completed this exchange when a tall, handsome woman in a nursing sister's uniform walked briskly toward them.

"Good morning, ladies. I'm Matron Elizabeth Harrison. What you've undertaken is far from easy, but I believe you are all well qualified to take on this challenge or you would not have been sent here by your supervisors. We run a tight ship here, but we're supportive of each other and work as a team. We expect discipline, strict adherence to duty, and unquestioned obedience to orders. I commend you for your patriotism."

Her bright eyes traveled over the group, and she gave a little nod. "You will be assigned two to a room, so choose your roommates, and settle in. Shift assignments will be posted as soon as you report to your ward nurse. Thank you, ladies." With that, she turned and walked back down the hall.

There was a moment of silence when they looked at each

other before Dora arranged the painting. "Let's go find our room, Kitty."

The Chateau Rougeret, once the palatial home of a noble family, had been transformed into a model British field hospital. On their way through the great halls, where patients lay on cots lining the walls, Kitty could see that most of the rooms had been converted into spaces accommodating four patients each. The staff, the VADs, and ambulance drivers were billeted to the top floor, which had once been the Rougeret servants' quarters.

At the top of what felt like thousands of stone steps up a twisting stairway, Kitty and Dora found the room they were to share. It was hardly more than a closet. As they unpacked, they bumped into each other repeatedly, at length bursting into helpless laughter.

"I don't mind telling you," Dora admitted, "I'm scared stiff! I've never tended war injuries before."

It was a relief to Kitty to put into words what they both were feeling.

After a cold supper taken in the staff dining room where they were barely acknowledged by weary nurses just coming off duty, they returned to their room. They got ready for bed quietly. Soon both were in their narrow cots, too absorbed in their own thoughts for further conversation.

Awakening well before 4:00 A.M., the hour she was to report for duty, Kitty left her cot and began to dress. She had not slept well. She had been too cold, for one thing, and too apprehensive, for another. Her fingers were numb as she buttoned on her coverall apron, laced up her shoes, adjusted her cap with its crisp veil, and pinned it in place.

As she dressed, all her self-doubts rose to taunt her, the questions pouncing upon her from the deep well of her own insecurities. Would she measure up to the Matron's expectations? Had her training at a civilian hospital equipped her to handle the kinds of wounds and injuries she would soon be seeing?

Dora was sleepy but cheerful when she finally joined Kitty in the dining room for a breakfast of coffee and chunks of toasted French bread. Except for a few sips of the scalding brew, however, Kitty could not swallow a thing.

When Dora left to receive her assignment in another ward, Kitty met the kind-eyed woman who would be her immediate supervisor. "Welcome, Nurse Cameron. I'm Sister Ferris."

She began by reviewing the duties Kitty would be expected to perform, showing her where supplies were kept and apprising her of daily routines and schedules. In response, Kitty warmed to her gentle instruction, feeling a returning of self-confidence.

Kitty soon learned that everyone admired Sister Ferris. She issued orders in a soft but authoritative voice and knew how to correct in a quiet manner, suggesting alternative tasks. Consequently, Sister Ferris was a favorite, adored and respected by doctors, nurses, and orderlies alike.

At the end of the day, Kitty found that Dora had not been so lucky. Her roommate had drawn a real tyrant for a ward nurse and soon came in at night, smarting from sharp reprimands, or reporting some hilarious encounter.

There was little time for the new group of VADs to become acclimated, for the first week, a big drive at the front brought a convoy of ambulances pouring into the courtyard. They came at night, the only time vehicles could safely transport the wounded without being the sure targets of enemy fire.

Nothing Kitty had yet experienced had prepared her for this carnage. As ambulance after ambulance deposited its victims, a barrage of moans and sharp outcries assaulted her ears. The sight of so much human suffering was permanently imprinted on her brain—the pain-contorted faces, the cries of agony, the panicked pleas for help.

Kitty and the other nurses did their best to handle the wounded as gently as possible, cutting off mud- and blood-soaked uniforms and making the men comfortable until a doctor could make a diagnosis and determine the treatment needed.

Up and down the crowded aisles they raced—from the hissing sterilizer to the bandage store to the sinks for antiseptic soap. From the operating room annex next to the ward, the odor of disinfectant and ether drifted in, making Kitty's nostrils prickle and making her stomach lurch uneasily.

Still, despite the grim realities she was facing, she was determined to remain calm, not become maudlin or ineffective. More than anything now, she wanted to become a highly skilled professional without losing her compassion.

For all her own discomfort, Kitty knew the suffering of these men was far more intense. Many of them had lain out in the cold and rain for hours, waiting to be picked up and driven to the hospital under the cover of darkness. So besides shrapnel wounds, the nurses soon began to see gangrene of the extremities, the result of standing knee-deep in muddy trenches, and dozens of cases of pneumonia and bronchitis from the abominable winter weather.

The painkillers and narcotics, kept under lock and key in the pharmacy, were reserved for the post-operative and amputation patients, so there was little to do for the others except rely on the remedies Kitty had learned in her Red Cross First Aid training—rub the feet and legs with oil, wrap them in soft cotton wool, and apply linseed poultices to the chest cases.

Kitty prayed as she worked, grateful for the skills she had

been taught that could alleviate even in small ways the agony of these men. The fact that they were all so grateful, often even apologetic for the trouble they were causing, humbled her, knowing how much more they had given.

The bone-chilling cold Kitty had noticed the first day never abated. At one time or another, almost all the staff succumbed to coughs or colds. But as long as the nurses could stay on their feet, there was no thought of taking a well-earned day off.

To make matters even worse, the weather turned really miserable—the coldest winter in fifty years—so said the French orderlies and ambulance drivers. Dora wrote her mother to send woolen long-johns, and a package from Blythe, containing beautifully knit sweaters, finally reached Kitty.

The added layers helped a little, but crawling out from the blankets on chill mornings became harder and harder. They dressed quickly, shivering convulsively, their breath frosty plumes in the frigid air.

After being on duty for twenty hours at a time, the long climb up the steep stone steps seemed an impossible challenge. Only the prospect of a few hours of dead sleep enabled Kitty to put one foot in front of the other.

In her room at the end of a day on the wards, Kitty was usually too physically drained to think about Kip. Not until she was finally in bed at night or had awakened in the eerie light of dawn, did her thoughts center on him. She had hoped to hear from him after she sent her letter telling him that she was now stationed in France. She hoped that he would find a way to come see her. Of course, she didn't know exactly where he was, or whether her letter had reached him. He might have been transferred to another airfield, or . . . and a deep shudder would tremble through her body. Surely if anything had happened to him, she would *know!*

Often Kitty had to fight the waves of homesickness that sometimes unexpectedly engulfed her. It was a kind of agonized aching for all the faraway beauty of Virginia, especially the blossoming woods between her home and Montclair where their little honeymoon house, Eden Cottage, awaited their return. The pink impatiens she had planted all along the flagstone path to the blue-painted door, seemed an almost comical reminder of a virtue she herself must cultivate.

Remembering it all, Kitty would close her eyes, feeling the awful urge to cry—for all the lost days, the lost happiness, the lost innocence before she had known about war and blood and the terrible dailiness of death.

chapter
16

In February came the news that after the sinking of an American freighter, the *Housatonic*, by a German submarine, President Wilson had broken off diplomatic relations with Germany. "Surely now the Americans will come in" was the opinion voiced most often by members of the medical staff at the chateau. But when weeks went by with no further word that the United States would join the Allies, Kitty and some of the other Americans attached to the British Red Cross unit felt an undercurrent of hostility beginning to surface.

Later in the month, a brutal German attack on Verdun sent the number of casualties soaring into the hundreds of thousands on both sides, and the staff was taxed to the utmost. News of the fierce battle brought an urgent demand for more ambulances to bring the wounded to the hospital. French as well as British units were alerted for service.

Soon a steady stream of ambulances was arriving at the chateau. To Kitty's mingled delight and dismay, knowing the risks of such duty, Cara was one of the drivers. The twins had a brief ecstatic reunion before the orders for dispatch were announced.

Since a VAD would be assigned to each ambulance, Kitty kept track of the posted assignments. When she saw that another VAD had been given the number of Cara's vehicle, Kitty quickly traded with her.

As they hurried out into the darkness and scrambled into the high cab of the ambulance, Cara spoke for the first time. "Thank God, there's no moon." She did not need to explain. Kitty understood her sister's remark. It was more than a statement. It was a heartfelt prayer of gratitude. Both knew that the Red Cross symbol painted on the top was not always the international protection it was designed to be, but at least the moonless night would give them a chance to move undetected past enemy fire.

If either twin had been struck by the incongruity of their presence here in France, neither said so. Only a year ago, that they should be setting out on such a mission would have seemed incredible.

Cara turned the vehicle expertly out into the line of ambulances. Kitty, sitting silent beside her, was gripped with anxiety. Was she up to what would be demanded of her before this night was over? She glanced over at her twin hunched over the wheel, saw her profile under the beaked cap—the small chin thrust out, her lips tightly compressed.

They drove through the night, in convoy, following the other three ambulances in front of theirs. Kitty felt her palms grow sweaty inside the woolen gloves. She squinted through the grimy windshield at the narrow winding road ahead.

When the signal came to stop, Cara slid into low gear and braked. The dull thud of bombs could be heard constantly in the distance now. Then came the whine followed by an explosion, and the sky lighted up for a split-second.

Kitty's stomach cramped, her heart banging against her ribs. *I'll never get used to it,* she thought, wondering how many men had been hit by that last shell.

They remained parked, waiting for another signal to move

forward. Sitting in tense silence, they heard the dull shuffling sound of marching boots.

As the men in the trenches were relieved, columns of weary soldiers trudged by on either side of the road. They moved like sleepwalkers, shoulders bent beneath heavy packs and guns, not talking, not looking to right or left. Their faces—haggard and gray, eyes glazed—mirrored the horror and hopelessness of all they had endured.

Kitty had never felt so frightened, so filled with defeat. Were the Allies losing the war?

Hearing a rustling noise, she turned to see several of the men leaving the ranks and falling wearily to the ground. Where were their officers? Was the whole army in retreat?

Just then Kitty heard Cara mumble something under her breath. She could not make out the words but knew that her sister was echoing her own reaction. What was it all for? She reached over and pressed Cara's hand. There was no need for words.

They waited tensely. There was a stirring of activity, felt rather than observed. A soldier moved alongside the line of ambulances, motioning them forward. Kitty felt her stomach muscles contract as Cara moved her foot alternately from accelerator to brake, struggling to steer the vehicle straight ahead, fearful that one of the men, blinded by exhaustion, might stumble under the wheels.

At a short blast from a whistle, Cara jammed on the brakes and the ambulance came to an abrupt stop. There was movement, low voices. Through the murky darkness, they could see figures emerging from the woods—medical corpsmen bringing out stretchers bearing wounded men.

Kitty jumped out, aware that Cara's orders were to remain at the wheel, ready to get going at a moment's notice if the bombardment started again.

Amid the cries of the injured, Kitty helped the stretcher-bearers load the ambulance. Quickly, and as gently as possible, they laid the men on the double layer of benches inside. Kitty spoke soothingly, assuring those who were conscious enough to understand, that they were on their way to help.

The ride back to the chateau was a nightmare. Every rut and bump and shell hole in the road brought fresh cries from the wounded men. Kitty bit her lip, holding onto the railing of the back door as the vehicle rocked back and forth.

When the torturous ride ended at the chateau, the waiting staff helped unload the men and made quick judgments as to which wards they should go for treatment. Kitty had no time to speak again to Cara but went directly on duty, helping with those assigned to her ward.

The activity was frantic. Uniforms had to be removed or cut away, the wounds washed and loosely bandaged, at least until the doctors could make their own examinations.

It was early morning before Kitty was relieved. Numb with fatigue, she staggered dizzily into the staff dining room to gulp down some strong, sweet tea.

When she asked about the ambulance drivers, she was told they had gone back for another run. But she knew the chateau had reached its capacity, and that the next load would be taken to another field hospital. Kitty felt a wave of sadness. She had not even had a chance to tell Cara good-bye. Nor did she know when . . . or if . . . they would see each other again.

chapter
17

WITH THE ADVENT of spring, the German flyers became more daring. Even in daytime, they flew so low over the chateau that the black cross on each wing was clearly visible. But it was at night when the moon was cruelly bright that they returned to dispatch their deadly bombs. Able to find their targets in its cold light, the pilots flew low. First, there would be a roar of engines, then a whistling whine, followed by a deafening explosion.

On such nights Kitty wondered why she had ever loved the moonlight, thought it romantic! For at last she was beginning to understand war, the wanton waste of it—the dead or damaged, the destruction of homes and land, the women and children deprived of husbands and fathers. When would it all end?

One afternoon while she was out for a rare breath of fresh air, Kitty saw a German plane meet its fate. It must have been returning after dropping its load of bombs, she decided, since the sound of its engine was different from those on the way to a bombing raid.

On the edge of the woods, she stopped to listen, looked up at the sky, and saw the plane with its recognizable insignia come into sight. Then she heard the rackety sound of anti-aircraft artillery. A minute later a red flame cut through the clouds almost directly above. The plane spiraled down in a spinning rocket of fire and disappeared. She held her breath, waiting for the muffled explosion.

Rooted to the ground, Kitty began to shake. She could picture the young man pinned in the horrible inferno of the crash. What if that had been Kip instead of the German pilot?

In the next few weeks, a shocking rumor began to circulate that the Germans were using poison gas. At first, no one believed it. Then the rumor was verified. Against all international law, the Germans had sent clouds of poison against the Allied troops with no other purpose than to inflict cruel suffering and death. Kitty was stunned.

At first, the only protection against the noxious fumes was primitive—squares of folded gauze, soaked in some sort of solution and tied with tapes around mouth and nose. Since these had to be kept moist to fit, the soldiers were forced to use polluted water from the trenches. Even then, the gas could seep in around the contrived masks. It was the ultimate in the war's degradation.

When the first victims came pouring into the hospital, writhing in pain, their lungs seared from the exploding fumes they had inhaled, Kitty's rage knew no bounds. When she was assigned to the German prisoner ward, going on duty became a daily test of will.

Kitty fought her anger for a government that would conceive and implement such a demonic weapon. As a nurse, however, her compassion extended to any soldier whose wounds she dressed. It was difficult to know when one emotion left off and another took its place. They were, after all, the enemy. Men who if, given the chance, were pledged to kill those she loved—Kip and all the others.

Not only that, but Kitty could see the ongoing questions in the eyes of her fellow nurses. Why didn't America—rich, powerful, strong—come in and help before it was too late?

She buried her own wondering. As a Christian, she must not hate. She must somehow forgive her own country for their failures, and she must learn to love her enemies, "do good" to those who persecuted her. So she surrendered to backbreaking work, stumbling exhaustion, and sleepless nights until she was too numb to feel.

In April America declared war on Germany. Shortly after that Kitty learned that Scott was in England, had seen Aunt Garnet and would soon be in France. Daily she expected some words from him.

One afternoon, just as she was finishing her shift, the matron sent for her. "You have a visitor, Cameron."

"It must be my brother!" Kitty exclaimed.

"Oh?" Matron lifted a skeptical eyebrow. "Most say they're *cousins*."

Kitty tried not to laugh, wondering how many times her supervisor had heard that likely story.

"Well, take the rest of the afternoon off, Cameron," she was told and rushed off before Matron could change her mind.

At the main entrance she saw Scott, looking fit and trim in a natty United States Army officer's uniform.

"Scott!" she cried and was caught up in a bear hug. "How marvelous to see you!"

"You, too, little sister!" He held her at arm's length. "Just look at you! How professional you look, but much too thin and pale. I'm going to kidnap you and make sure you have a square meal. Can you get some time off?"

"Only a few hours—"

"Try for longer. I've requisitioned a vehicle. We can drive

up to Paris. I'd planned to take you to one of the finest restaurants, force some of those delectable French pastries on you. Surely your commanding officer would allow you to spend some time with a long-lost brother!"

Kitty was dubious. "I'll see, but you don't know Matron—"

"Shall I pull rank?" Scott struck a Napoleonic stance.

She grinned in spite of her fatigue. All at once, she felt younger, freer than she had in ages. It *would* be good to get away, catch up on old times. "I'll ask. All she can do is say no, right?"

When Kitty returned to her ward, Matron looked up from a batch of reports on her office desk and gave Kitty a long thoughtful look. "I realize this is a special occasion, Cameron, but I can only grant you a short leave. You know the situation here." She made a notation on a chart, then said brusquely, "Twenty-four hours—no more."

Paris, even in wartime, still held its legendary magic. Driving up the tree-lined boulevard into the center of the city, Kitty's spirits lifted. Although damp and cold at this time of year, the city was all she had imagined it would be—the Champs Elysees, the Eiffel Tower soaring against the gray sky, the Arc de Triomphe, reminding her of a victorious ending of another war.

They left the requisitioned vehicle at army headquarters, once a luxury hotel, and started off on foot. There was so much to see. The sidewalks were filled with people strolling, most of them in uniform. Many were Americans, looking healthy and vigorous in comparison to some of the British and French officers. After all, she realized with a pang of guilt, the Americans had not been fighting a seemingly invincible enemy for four long years.

158

To Kitty's amazement, the shop windows were filled with all sorts of items. There seemed no shortages or lack of any kind. Upon closer inspection, however, she could see that the displays consisted mostly of luxuries—"haute couture" fashions, beaded purses, feathered hats, jewelry, leather goods.

Still, it was fun to see all the lovely things. Kitty could almost forget why she and Scott were in this city, so far from home.

"Tired?" he asked when they had spent an hour sight-seeing and window shopping.

"Not really!"

"I'm sure you've worked up an appetite by now. You're way too thin, you know, Kit," he commented in a concerned, big-brotherly tone. "Shall we find that restaurant now?"

"I'm not about to turn you down. Not after my steady diet of hospital food." She took Scott's arm. "Ready any time you are."

"One of the attachés in our unit gave me the name of a place he says offers the epitome in French cuisine. So I think we should head in that direction." Scott paused to study a street sign. "It's quite near here, I think."

"Fine. We can do some more touristing after we eat."

They had just crossed the street and were walking down the sidewalk when Kitty stopped abruptly. Her hand tightened on Scott's arm. Puzzled, he halted, glancing at his sister, who had turned suddenly pale. Then he looked in the direction she was staring.

Kip Montrose! Scott almost called his name until he saw that Kip was not alone. He was coming out of a hotel, arm in arm with a young woman wearing the gray-blue uniform of a French ambulance driver. They were laughing, her face turned up toward his. Scott turned to look at Kitty and saw his sister's stricken expression.

Kitty stood motionless, unable to believe her eyes. At a glance, she took in the woman's dark sparkling eyes, the rosy-red mouth, the dark hair cut in a straight bang across her forehead. But it was the radiant look on her face rather than her beauty that struck Kitty. She recognized that look. It was the look of a woman in love.

For a minute Kitty couldn't breathe. Her fingers dug into Scott's arm. Instinctively, she stepped back so that her brother's body shielded her from view in case Kip should turn and see them.

But Kip was much too involved in his conversation with the girl on his arm to be aware that anyone else existed. Still laughing, he hailed a taxi and, when it drew up at the curb, he handed his companion inside and hopped in after her. Then the cab pulled away and rolled down the street.

Kitty remained transfixed, her face chalk-white, her eyes reflecting her bewilderment and hurt.

"I'm sorry, Kitty—" Scott began.

"Don't," she ordered from between clenched teeth. "Don't. Please just don't say anything."

Slowly they resumed walking down the street and into the first café.

The Café D'Auberge was bustling with activity. Nurses were identifiable by their white veils, the red cross emblazoned on the headband. They sat at tables across from aviators in leather jackets. Mixed with the sound of voices and laughter was their determined air of seizing this moment.

Other couples in various types of uniforms were enjoying a brief respite from wartime danger and anxiety. Scott found a table for two in the corner.

Kitty stared fixedly into space. Scott's attempts at conversation failed miserably, and they sat in numbed silence until a mustachioed waiter came to take their order.

"Two brandies."

When Kitty protested, Scott said firmly, "For medicinal purposes. You're in shock." He put his hand over her small one. "Kitty, it's wartime. A man like Kip—"

She stopped him with an upraised hand. "Don't make excuses for him, Scott. I don't need that. I just need some time to absorb what's happened—"

Kitty *was* in shock. But the brandy did not help. Nor did the genuine sympathy in Scott's eyes or his insistence that she eat every bite of the succulent *coque au vin* the waiter set before her.

Afterward they drove from Paris back through the dark countryside. Sitting beside her brother, still unable to speak, Kitty looked up at the stars and at the tall trees that lined the road like sentinels. She wondered if, when the numbness wore off, would she feel unbearable pain? How long would it take her to get over Kip?

When they reached the chateau, Scott got out of the car, came around and helped Kitty out. Then he put his arms around her, cradling her head against his shoulder. "I'm so sorry, little sister."

Kitty shook her head. "No, Scott. I knew ... I *felt* something was wrong. I have for weeks. I just wouldn't admit it to myself. It's been ages since I heard from Kip even though he knew I was here. If he could get leave to go to Paris ... he could have come here, if he'd wanted to. No, I've just been denying it."

Scott tried again. "Maybe there's some explanation—"

A rush of emotion threatened to overwhelm Kitty, but she managed to say, "I'm only sorry it spoiled our day together."

"It didn't, not really. It was wonderful to be with you, Kitty." Scott's voice was husky. "I'll try to get another leave. I'm not sure where the colonel will be sent, but of course, I'll have to go with him. So good-bye for now. And . . . take care."

He hugged Kitty hard, wishing with all his heart he could have spared her today's heartbreak, wishing also that he could keep her safe from the horrors to which she was returning.

The letter that Kitty had anticipated but dreaded came a few weeks later. She recognized Kip's familiar scrawl immediately but sat holding the envelope, postponing the inevitable. Even so, it was a shock to see the truth in writing.

"I would give anything not to have to write this, Kitty," Kip began.

> I know this is going to hurt. . . . But I've fallen in love with a wonderful French girl. Her name is Etienette Boulanger. She's an ambulance driver and, strangely enough, thinks she has met Cara. Small world, eh?
>
> If circumstances were different, I know you'd like her. She's everything we've always admired—courageous, fun-loving, good. We've know each other only a short time, but we're very sure it's right. We're going to be married in her village church. She's at home now telling her family, and I'll follow in a few days as soon as my leave is approved.

For a long, desolate time, Kitty sat immobilized. Then the letter dropped from her fingers, and she buried her face in her hands.

She was still sitting on the edge of her bed when Dora came into the room from her shift. "You're due on the ward, Kitty. Better hurry. Matron's in a foul mood." She hardly glanced in Kitty's direction, but flopped wearily onto her cot, dragged up her blanket, and closed her eyes.

With effort, Kitty got to her feet. She reached for her apron, buttoned it, put on her headband and veil and left the room. She moved along the corridor and down the steps like an automaton. Signing in on the duty chart, she made her rounds, attending to her patients, all the time trying to make some sense of what had happened.

It all seemed so pointless now. Despite her growing nursing skill, Kip was the reason she had come here in the first place. He was the reason for everything, the driving force that made it possible to put up with all this hellish life—the blood, the mud, the never-ending cold, the boom of guns. If it were not for her love for Kip, she would be safely home in Virginia right now—

Now everything had come crashing in around her. After everything she had hoped and dreamed all these years, Kip loved someone else, someone he had just met, a *stranger*. And he was going to marry her—

But in her heart Kitty knew that there were other reasons she had come to this place. There must be! She was becoming a better nurse. She was doing some good, wasn't she? In spite of what had happened, in spite of Kip, she had to believe that.

Work was Kitty's anesthetic. Still, she dreaded the moment it would wear off, no longer able to kill the pain. In her nursing duties with the amputees, she had heard the doctors talk about "phantom pain," the kind suffered after amputation. Even when a damaged limb was removed, patients complained of feeling pain in it and begged for something to stop it. But there was no one, nothing to stop the pain for Kitty.

After that day in Paris, after Kip's letter, Kitty moved through her days relying on her training, her instincts to do her job. But a part of her mind was always preoccupied with what had happened to her dreams. Ever since Kip had left to join the French Flying Corps, Kitty's thoughts were *after the war, when Kip and I* will do this or that. Now there was only the "I." She had no idea what she would do with the rest of her life.

Coming off her shift one afternoon, Kitty went to her room for a much-needed nap. As she started to remove her headband, it caught on a hairpin and held fast. She tugged at it irritably but, as she did, pulled out more hairpins, and her hair tumbled down onto her shoulders.

Impulsively she reached into her apron pocket for her surgical scissors, grabbed a handful of hair, and whacked it off. It hung there in a jagged clump.

Suddenly the realization of what she had done struck Kitty. She stared into the small wavy mirror above the bureau. One side of her hair was cut off below her ear, the rest fell nearly to her waist. What should she do now?

Just then Dora came in off duty, saw her, and gasped. "Good grief, Kitty! Are you out of your mind?"

"No, I had an uncontrollable urge, that's all." Kitty turned around to face her roommate, then put on a pitiable face. "Help!"

"Oh, Kitty!" Dora moaned. "Your beautiful hair!"

"Cut the rest of it off for me, will you, please?"

"Oh, no, Kitty! Don't ask me to do that!"

"You'll have to. I can't leave it like this." Kitty held out the scissors.

Reluctantly Dora took them and began to cut.

"Shorter," Kitty ordered.

"Shorter?"

"Yes." Kitty's voice was firm.

"Well, you've got naturally curly hair at least, and it's such a lovely color. Besides," Dora continued philosophically, "your cap and veil will cover most of it."

But Kitty eyed her newly cropped head sadly. It was a far

cry from the sleek, dark "bobbed" cap of hair she had seen on Etienette Boulanger.

Still, her rash decision had achieved something else. Something important. She wasn't quite sure why, but she felt as different as she looked. It was as if cutting off her hair had freed her in some strange way.

Part V

Keep the home fires burning,
Though the hearts are yearning,
Turn those dark clouds inside out
Till the boys come home.
                    —a popular song of 1917

chapter
18

Mayfield, Virginia
Late Summer 1917 at Cameron Hall

"WHEN WILL THE war be over, Gran?" Lynette asked Blythe.

"I wish I knew, darling." Blythe glanced up from the letter she was reading and looked fondly at her little granddaughter and beyond to the lovely sweep of lawn. The hydrangeas were in full bloom and a soft breeze gently stirred the leaves of the trees that shaded the veranda where they were sitting. On this mid-summer afternoon, here in the peaceful Virginia countryside, it was hard to imagine a war raging on the other side of the world. "We must just keep praying it will end soon."

The little girl nodded earnestly. "I do. Every night."

Blythe sighed. All three of her Cameron children were in the thick of it—Scott, stationed in Paris, which was constantly threatened by German invasion; Cara and Kitty, near the front lines.

As if reading her grandmother's thoughts, Lynette said plaintively, "I miss Kitty very much. She doesn't even know I've learned to jump and am riding a horse instead of a pony now."

"Why don't you write her a letter and tell her so? Better still, why don't you draw her a picture of yourself on Princess, going over the stone wall at the end of the driveway? I know she'd love that."

"What a good idea, Gran. I'll go get my crayons."

Blythe smiled as the child scrambled up and ran into the house. Her granddaughter was really quite talented artistically. She wished that Jeff noticed her more, encouraged her. Even after six years, he was not yet over Faith's tragic death. Sadly, he seemed to have lost interest in everything—his children, his art, even life itself.

Blythe sighed again, this time a sigh so deep it was almost painful. All she had ever wanted for her children was happiness, but now all of their lives had been touched by some deep tragedy—Jeff's wife's death, Kitty's broken engagement, and now Cara.

She dreaded writing Scott the latest news that Cara's husband, Owen Brandt, had been killed in action. He had died while bringing a wounded soldier to safety from the battlefield. Of course, the fact that he had died a hero wouldn't ease the young widow's sorrow or make his death any easier to bear.

Between the lines of Scott's letter, Blythe sensed *his* heart's loneliness, for Scott had not yet found a love of his own. She read the poignant last paragraph of her son's letter:

To keep myself sane, I try to remember what it was like as short a time ago as summer before last. In my mind, I see the smooth, green lawn where we used to play croquet, the men in their blue blazers and white flannels, the girls in fluffy white dresses . . . flowers everywhere . . . eating strawberries and drinking iced lemonade by the gallon . . . I'm thirsty for it all!

And I think about the twins a great deal. How alike they were and yet how different . . . their glossy curls bobbing, the sound of

170

their giggles. And somewhere there is music . . . there always seems to be music in my dreams . . . and Kitty's sweet face, her eyes—and Cara dancing . . .

Well, Cara isn't dancing now. Would she ever want to dance again? Blythe remembered her own young widowhood and prayed Cara would not grieve too long or too irreconcilably. She was still young enough to find another love, begin a new life. And Kitty, what about dear Kitty?

* * *

Somewhere in France

Chateau Rougeret Hosptial
December 1917

The strains of "Minuit Chritiens" echoed from the small chapel where midnight services were being held for the Catholic members of the hospital staff. Listening to the clear voices ringing out onto the crisp night air, Kitty hummed along with the melody, mentally substituting for the French words the familiar English ones: "O holy night, the stars are brightly shining./It is the night of the dear Savior's birth—"

Earlier she had left the scene of New Year's Eve merrymaking in the staff room. It had seemed so artificial, so forced that, overcome with emotion, she had felt the need to escape. Throwing her cape around her shoulders, Kitty went out into the starry night to walk along the stone terrace of the chateau.

Out here it was as still as it might have been that long-ago night in Bethlehem. For once the guns were silent. It seemed so peaceful that one could almost forget—but that was an illusion. There was no peace, although it was rumored that the Germans were as desperate for it as the Allies. There was even a report that on Christmas Eve, both the German and French soldiers had joined in singing "Silent Night" in their own language from their trenches.

How much longer could this dreadful war go on?

Kitty thought of the poem Richard Traherne had enclosed in a recent letter:

> *The snow is falling softly on the earth,*
> *Grown hushed beneath its covering of white;*
> *O Father, let another peace descend*
> *On all of troubled hearts this winter night.*
>
> *Look down upon them in their anxious dark,*
> *On those who sleep not for their fear and care,*
> *On those with tremulous prayers on their lips,*
> *The prayers that stand between them and despair.*
>
> *Let fall Thy comfort as this soundless snow:*
> *Make troubled hearts aware in Thine own way*
> *Of love beside them in this quiet hour,*
> *Of strength with which to meet the coming day.*

The enclosure had seemed so timely. Just that morning she had been reading in her small devotional book, trying to snatch a scrap of serenity before going on duty. The Scripture for meditation had been John 14:27: "Let not your heart be troubled, neither let it be afraid."

What a coincidence! Kitty thought when she received Richard's letter with the poem that same afternoon. It was almost as if he had sensed her discouragement and fear.

But then Richard was very perceptive. Ever since Birchfields last year, he had written to her occasionally, friendly letters, often enclosing poetry or some quotation from a newspaper or magazine. Then a few weeks ago, she had a letter from him saying he had met Scott in Paris and had been so pleased to hear news of her. Kitty could not help wondering if her brother had told him about her broken engagement.

She checked her watch. It was nearly midnight. Maybe she should go back inside and try to blend in with the others, find a little joy in whatever time was left.

The party was still going strong when Kitty entered the staff room. Twisted lengths of faded red and green crepe paper festooned the walls where a big sign had been hung proclaiming in tarnished gilt letters: "HAPPY NEW YEAR! WELCOME 1918!"

The small group remaining had formed a circle, and someone was trying to find the right pitch for "Auld Lang Syne." Seeing Kitty, a VAD broke the circle and made room for her. She moved forward, clasping her hand on one side, the hand of an orderly on the other.

"Should auld acquaintance be forgot and never brought to mind—" sang a mixed chorus of voices. Kitty found it difficult to sing with the hard lump in her throat. Memories of other New Year's Eves back home at Cameron Hall flooded her mind. She had welcomed most of them with Kip. How many New Year's Eves would she have to greet without him?

The song ended with a round of cheers and applause. Then with an exchange of greetings, hugs, and kisses, some departed to go back on duty. In a few minutes another group just finishing their shift, straggled into the staff room. This bunch did not linger, their slumped shoulders and heavy-lidded eyes proclaiming their need for sleep more than holiday cheer. One by one, they left. Everyone, that is, except Dora, who insisted on helping with the cleanup.

The two began gathering up tattered streamers and

discarded poppers, then collected glasses and cups, carrying them out to the adjoining kitchen.

"Dora, I can manage here. You go on up to bed," Kitty suggested. "You've already worked a full shift and must be tired. I don't go on until seven A.M."

"I *am* beat," admitted Dora, stifling a yawn. "Are you sure you don't mind?"

"Positive. I'm not sleepy at all. And this won't take long."

"Well, if you're sure—" She eyed the clutter, the dirty dishes still to be washed.

"Dora!" Kitty shooed her off. "Do go on."

When her roommate left, Kitty stacked the dishes and cups, waiting while the water heated. She was pouring liquid soap into the sink, stirring it with her hands into sud when she heard a movement behind her. Thinking that Dora had returned, feeling guilty for leaving her with the work.

Without looking, Kitty called over her shoulder. "Dora, I meant it! Go along to bed! What's it going to take to convince you I can handle—"

She half-turned her head to confront her. But instead of Dora, there was Richard Traherne standing in the doorway.

She whirled around. "*Richard!* What in the world are you doing here?"

"Is that any way to greet a fellow who's driven three hours straight across the worst roads imaginable to wish you a Happy New Year?" he demanded, smiling.

"But—but—" she stammered. "Of course, it's wonderful to see you, but how did you manage it?"

"The colonel decided to see the new year in with some friends in the country not far from here, so I drove him over." He grinned. "Then he gave me leave to spend the rest of the holiday as I like." He came toward her, holding out both hands.

174

"Oh, I'm all soapy," she apologized, starting to wipe her hands on her skirt.

"Never mind. I won't shake hands. I'll just kiss you instead. Happy New Year, Kitty." His lips brushed hers lightly, then he looked down at her, regarding her. "It's so *good* to see you again."

"And you, Richard," Kitty murmured, knowing it was true. "I've appreciated your letters so much. Especially the poetry." She looked into his eyes and felt a kind of joy welling up inside.

His eyes moved over her as if taking inventory. "You've cut your hair . . . your beautiful hair! But I think I like it. It suits you."

She ran her hand through the crop of curls. "It's ever so comfortable and convenient." Feeling a little self-conscious under his admiring gaze, she asked rather breathlessly, "Are you starved? We've been having a party and there's plenty of cake left . . . and I can make some cocoa—"

"Sounds just right, Kitty. Reminds me of the homey feeling of coming into a warm kitchen and sitting down at the kitchen table after a day of ice-skating or sledding."

She laughed gaily. "It will only take a minute!"

Richard watched her reflectively. Although she was thinner than he remembered, there was a new sort of grace about her as she moved about, pouring milk into a saucepan, spooning in the powdered chocolate. As she turned to look at him, he was struck by the fact that in spite of what she must have endured, Kitty had a kind of innocence, a purity that remained untouched. A hope he had tried to banish came alive in him again. After all, her brother *had* told him she was no longer engaged to the childhood sweetheart back home. Dare he risk another rejection?

Kitty arranged a tray with two mugs, a beverage server, a

plate with slices of the dark, rich fruitcake that Dora's mother had sent them. "Come along, we'll go into the staff room. We even have a little decorated tree in there, and we might as well enjoy it."

"Let me carry that." Richard took the tray from her, then followed as she led the way, setting it down on one of the tables.

Kitty proceeded to pour the cocoa. "Here you are." She placed the mug before him, its chocolaty steam rising tantalizingly, then poured herself a mug and sat down opposite him.

Richard felt his heart lift recklessly. How lovely she was— the warm brown eyes with their direct gaze, the curve of her cheek, the compassionate mouth. Even in the ugly gunmetal-gray uniform, she had astonishing beauty.

They talked easily, like old friends unexpectedly reunited. She asked how he and Scott had met and learned that they had been stationed in the same Paris hotel, now the headquarters of the joint Allied communications team. After a few questions, Kitty was brought up to date on her brother, and they moved to other topics. Mostly they spoke of the past, of their lives before they had met at Birchfields.

Surprisingly, they found much more in common. Richard knew Cape Cod well, had summered at Martha's Vineyard with his grandparents as a little boy. He told her of losing his mother when he was ten, of boarding school, of school holidays. His grandfather had been a history professor at a small New England college, and Richard had been at the university when his father remarried. Although he was fond of his stepmother, the family was not close.

"I'm a little envious . . . your having such an extended family, I mean," Richard said. "My brother Brad is a

176

lieutenant in the U. S. navy now. But I haven't seen him since I enlisted in the Canadian army."

Kitty touched the double bars on his uniform jacket. "I see that you made captain."

"Yes . . . well, I wish the whole awful thing were over."

They were quiet for a minute, then Kitty held up her empty cup. "More?"

"No, thanks. But I see a gramophone over there. Would we disturb anyone if we played it?"

"Not at all. The wards are quite a distance from here, and the walls of the chateau are thick."

Richard got up and went over to look through the meager stack of records.

"They're all pretty scratchy, I'm afraid," Kitty told him. "They've been played so much."

He studied the labels, then cranked the handle and carefully put a record on the turntable. Then he was holding out his arms to her, and Kitty moved into them as the record began, spinning out the strains of "If you were the only girl in the world—"

Suddenly it was last Christmas at Birchfields, the scent of cedar, the soft glow of candles—

Richard's arm was around her waist, her hand in his. They moved as one, around and around, the music flowing over and through them in harmony.

Kitty felt Richard's lips on her hair, felt his fingers tighten on her hand, felt his arm drawing her closer. "Kitty, Kitty, if you only knew how often I've dreamed of this," he murmured.

The music stopped, but they went on dancing. Richard led her back to the gramophone and flipped the record to the other side. "I'm always chasing rainbows," the vocalist crooned.

"Is that what I'm doing, Kitty? Chasing rainbows?" Richard asked.

She looked up at him, not knowing quite what to say.

"Scott told me you're no longer engaged."

Kitty felt her face flame with remembered humiliation.

"Don't blame Scott for betraying a confidence. I asked him point-blank—" He paused. "Ever since Birchfields . . . well, I've never been able to get you out of my mind, Kitty. Is it too soon? Should I have kept quiet?"

"No, Richard, it's all right. Really. Of course, it hurt at the time . . . even now, when I know it's over, that he loves someone else. I guess I haven't dealt with the reality yet—" She shook her head. "I just go on from day to day, doing my work. . . . It's just that Kip was so much a part of my life . . . at least my life back home—"

She hesitated. "I've thought a lot about it and now realize it might have happened anyway after the war, when we were back in Virginia. We may have both changed, and it wouldn't be right for either of us anymore. It's better that it happened now before . . . well, before we made a worse mistake—"

"Come, let's sit down," Richard suggested. "There's much to talk about."

They found much to say to each other as the hours slipped by. Time passed, and still there was more. They never even noticed when the eerie gray of winter dawn crept through the narrow windows. It wasn't until a nurse came in for coffee before going on duty and snapped off the light switch, that they realized they had talked through the night.

Richard was all concern. "You'll be dead on your feet."

Kitty dismissed that and asked, "How much leave do you have?"

"I have to pick the colonel up tomorrow morning."

Kitty hesitated only briefly before suggesting, "What if I

ask Matron for the day off? I can take someone else's shift another day."

"Would you do that, Kitty? It would mean the world to me if we could spend the next twenty-four hours together."

"I think . . . I'm sure I can arrange it. Look, we'll both get a few hours' rest, then you come back for me at . . . three o'clock?"

At Kitty's request, there was a glimmer of amusement and understanding in Matron's eyes. She pursed her lips as if considering. "I wouldn't want you to make a habit of this, Cameron. But you *are* one of my best VADs, and you haven't had a day off in a long time. So, permission granted."

Richard was back promptly at three. He had rented a room at the village inn, and told Kitty that the innkeeper's wife had suggested he bring his "amie" back for dinner. "The villagers think you American and British nurses are *magnifique*. I told her I heartily agree, especially where *one* of them is concerned." He grinned. "But then I'm prejudiced."

Kitty had the grace to blush a little. "Let's walk, Richard. I hardly ever get a chance to be out in the fresh air." She fastened on her cape.

They started down the road from the chateau, stepping carefully over the frozen ruts, patches of snow still clinging to the hard brown winter ground. But the sky was a washed blue and the air was cold and sharp.

Kitty felt lightheaded and strangely invigorated. *Sleep deprivation,* she told herself with clinical objectivity. But when Richard took her hand and drew it through his arm, she felt a pleasant tingling sensation. They walked on, saying little, finding conversation unnecessary.

When they reached the village inn, Madame Julienne welcomed them. She beamed at Richard and fluttered over Kitty as she led them through the main restaurant to a secluded alcove. There a single table had been set at a window in a pool of winter sunshine.

After serving them a superb omelet and croissants still warm from the oven, Madame wished them "Bon appetit!" and left.

Kitty had not realized that she was so hungry and relished the delicious food, then pushed back her plate with a sigh. "That was the best meal I've had since . . . since I don't know when."

Richard poured her a cup of coffee from the white porcelain coffeepot. He added cream to his and stirred it slowly, gathering his thoughts, pacing his words. "You know I love you, Kitty. I've never stopped. Even when I thought there was no chance, I couldn't help myself."

He reached for her hand, brought it up to his lips, kissed her fingertips. "Maybe it's too soon, but time is so precious now. I have to know. Is there a chance? Could you give me some hope?"

Kitty returned his searching gaze. "I don't know, Richard. I honestly don't know. I wouldn't want to say yes and give you second-best, a rebound love."

Richard smiled. "I'll take whatever I can get, Kitty."

"But you're too good for that. Love should be so much more."

"That's what I'm trying to tell you. We don't have time for dwelling in the past, trying to make sense out of what happens. You and I . . . all of us in our generation . . . are caught up in this tangled web of history. We may not have a future. The world may blow itself up any day. Can't you see?" His grip tightened on her hand. "You do care for me, don't you, Kitty? At Birchfields you said you did. I don't think that's changed."

"I do *care* for you, Richard—" She paused. "It just seems to have happened so fast . . . I'm not sure—"

"Kitty, nothing in life is guaranteed. The only thing I'm sure of is that I love you. Let's be happy together for whatever time we have. Please say yes."

Richard's eyes were so full of tenderness that Kitty felt a stirring within her. She so wanted to return the devotion she saw there. But was that enough? Was it the kind of love he deserved? Or was it only gratitude for filling the aching void she had felt in the aftermath of heartbreak?

What Richard wanted was an enduring commitment. Marriage. Such a major decision in life had its consequences, Kitty knew, making a wartime wedding even more hazardous. She had to be honest with him and with herself. To tell Richard she loved him meant that she must pull away from the hold of the past . . . let Kip go.

She thought of the years stretching back to Virginia, to those she had dreamed of sharing with Kip at Eden Cottage. Then she thought of the years ahead, reaching into an unknown future . . . with Richard?

Looking again into his eyes, Kitty felt a warmth, a tenderness beginning to build within her. Why not accept this fine, honorable man's love, his desire to cherish and protect her? Suddenly it seemed so right. She smiled, and watched the anxiety in his eyes give way to hope.

"Kitty?"

"Yes, Richard, yes, if you're willing to take a chance—"

As soon as the words were out of her mouth, Kitty felt her heart leap. Maybe this marriage *was* a risk, particularly now in the middle of a war, but this kind of happiness was worth it. Hadn't someone said that love demands all, that one must not count the cost?

When they left the restaurant, they walked slowly past the

village and up the hill toward the hospital—still talking, saying all the things that people newly aware of each other say.

In sight of the chateau, Richard stopped and pointed to the arched cloister leading to the small Gothic building beside it. "What is that?"

"That's the chapel."

He regarded Kitty for a moment, his eyes thoughtful. "Let's see if it's open."

Surprised, Kitty hesitated. "Oh, I don't know if we should. I believe it's Madame Rougeret's private family chapel."

"It's God's house, isn't it?" Richard countered.

"Yes, I suppose—"

"Come on then." He took her hand.

The heavy, carved door squeaked as they pushed it open. Stepping inside, they blinked as their eyes became accustomed to the dim interior. There were no pews here, only chairs with racks on the back for prayerbooks. The room smelled of beeswax candles, of ancient stones and incense. Slowly, still holding hands, they moved quietly forward.

At the curved steps leading up to the altar there were a few wooden kneelers. Over the altar, a large brass crucifix gleamed in the shafts of light filtering down through the arched windows.

"Kitty, let's ask a blessing on our love, that it becomes what Scripture tells us it should be . . . whatever the future holds for us. I believe we've been given a special gift, and I just want to give thanks."

Richard was so serious, so sincere, that Kitty felt humbled, touched. Wordlessly she nodded, and they knelt down on the stone steps together and bowed their heads, praying silently.

At first Kitty's mind was a blank. Lately her prayers had been inarticulate cries for help—help for getting over Kip, for the men whose shattered bodies she was responsible for nursing back to health.

As she knelt beside Richard, her heart began to swell with gratitude. Richard had said they had been given a gift. Love was *always* a gift. And what does one do when one receives a gift? One says "Thank you." Kitty smiled at the simplicity of the revelation. Almost at once, words of thanksgiving rushed into her mind. They seemed childish, yet somehow she believed that God understood and was pleased. With one last plea for Richard's protection as he returned to the front, she got to her feet.

Hand in hand, they walked out of the chapel and back into the sunlight.

"Oh, Kitty, don't you think it's significant we started out this new year together?" Richard asked, taking her into his arms when it was time for him to leave. "Starting a brand-new life together, remembering all the rest of our lives that it began on New Year's Day 1918?"

Not until after Richard in a haze of happiness had given her one last lingering kiss and climbed back into the colonel's car, did Kitty have second thoughts. Not until much later did she wonder if her decision had been made in a moment of reckless euphoria.

No, wartime had nothing to do with it, Kitty argued with herself. She loved Richard and he loved her, deeply. If she had met him another time, another place, she would still have been attracted to him. Even last Christmas, with Kip still in the picture, she had found Richard charming, everything she admired in a man. After the war, they would have a wonderful, fulfilling life together—

Dora was enthusiastically happy for her when Kitty shared

the news. "What a looker your fellow is! You're a lucky girl, I'd say, Kitty."

That's what Kitty kept telling herself, too, when letters from Richard began to come regularly. Letters filled with loving concern, plans for their future, declarations of the joy her promise had given him. One day a small package arrived, containing an initialed gold signet ring Kitty had noticed on his little finger.

With it was a note:

Darling Kitty, This ring was my mother's. I want to set my seal on you so that none of those dashing doctors or patients who think you're the reincarnation of Florence Nightingale get any ideas! Wear it until the time we can pick out a proper engagement ring together at Tiffany's in New York or maybe in Paris, if you'll agree to marry me on my next leave!

Kitty could not wear the ring on her finger because her hands were too often in disinfectant or rubber gloves. Instead, she put it on a chain that she wore around her neck under her uniform, beside the little cross that Blythe had given her before she'd gone overseas. Feeling it there made her feel loved, cherished, protected, and helped banish any lingering doubts that she and Richard may have acted too hastily. Remembering their time in the chapel together comforted her. Surely the Lord had brought him into her life, hadn't He?

chapter
19

In MAY, the Allies—France, Britain, and now the United States—were united under one joint commander, the French General Foch, and there was growing optimism that the entrance of the American forces would turn the tide of the war.

There seemed no weakening of resolve within the German army, however, and hoping to crush the Allies before the full benefit of the American alliance could be felt, they mounted a huge campaign. By the end of the month they had reached the banks of the Marne River. Here they met resistance in the form of a brigade of American marines at Belleau Woods on the road to Paris.

Discussions of the war in the staff room were electrified. For Kitty it was a time of pride in her countrymen and dismay in the growing number of casualties. Now many Americans were among the wounded brought in by ambulance. It saddened her to see how young they were. Only a few short months ago they had been playing football on the high school team, going to proms, having sodas at the local drugstore with their sweethearts. Now they were dying.

A second fierce battle between the Americans and Germans took place at Chateau Thierry and there, by enormous effort,

American troops prevented the enemy from sweeping across the Marne into Paris. At this point, even Dr. Marchand, one of the French surgeons reputed to be an anti-American, favored Kitty with his version of a smile.

During July, five battles raged simultaneously, with news bulletins reporting the progress of the Allies posted each day in the staff room. Then in August, the fighting intensified.

One hot day, coming off duty, Kitty learned of an offensive led by Canadian and Australian troops deep into the enemy stronghold at Amiens. She felt her blood run cold. Was Richard involved? As an aide to the colonel in Communications, he might well be. *Oh, dear God, keep him safe!* she prayed, terrified.

A few days later she received several letters at once from him. But they were undated, hastily written, and gave her no comfort. She could do nothing but follow Paul's exhortation to "pray without ceasing" as she went about her duties.

The days dragged on. Early in September, Kitty was assigned to the ward for the hopelessly wounded. The French called it *Salle de Mort,* the "room of death." Patients remained here only a few days before being replaced by other terminal cases. There was little the nursing staff could do for them except keep them as comfortable as possible.

One of Kitty's most painful duties was to write letters home for some of these soldiers, often dictated in their dying breath. Of if there was no time, Kitty herself, hoping to spare some wife or mother the pain of an official notice, wrote to tell how nobly her loved one had fought and died for his country.

But more and more Kitty became sickened, her illusions shattered. War was not ennobling or glorious. It was horrible, useless!

The day she learned of Thax Collinwood's death, Kitty had just pulled the sheet over the face of a boy barely eighteen and had signaled the orderly to carry him out of the ward. Taking a brief break, she had checked her mail and found a letter from her mother.

"Thax and his commanding officer were standing at the top of their trench, getting a breath of air, when a shell landed nearby," Blythe wrote. "They were both killed instantly in the explosion."

Thax—always fun-loving, gracious, a considerate friend. He had enjoyed everything about life—theater, picnics, sailing . . . That his bright presence was gone, that she would never see his smile or listen to his latest funny story seemed impossible. Thax was part of her youth, of some of the happiest times of her life. How could he be gone?

Head down, choking back tears, she walked aimlessly, and found herself on the other side of the chapel in the garden that must have once been the showplace of the estate. Although now overgrown and neglected, its ornate Italian statuary chipped and broken where shells had fallen, the garden still had a certain forlorn beauty.

The day was unusually quiet, with a stillness that was in odd contrast to the turmoil within Kitty. She felt a hundred years old. What peace was possible in this war-torn world? Hot tears started, rolling helplessly down her cheeks.

Then from behind her a voice spoke. "*Tu est triste, mademoiselle?*"

Startled, Kitty wiped her eyes and turned around. Standing behind her in the shadows of the cloistered passageway was an elderly lady in black. Instinctively, she knew it must be Madame Rougeret.

Wondering if this part of the grounds was off-limits to hospital personnel and fearing that she might be trespassing, Kitty stood guiltily. "*Excusez-moi, Madame.*"

"*Non, mademoiselle, il n'y pas quoi.*" The woman shook her

head and made a gesture of dismissal with one graceful hand. Then in accented but perfect English, she continued, "Do not apologize for tears. They are God's gift to ease the pain of heartbreak. If you did not sometimes weep . . . with what you see every day . . . surely it would be more than one could bear."

Madame Rougeret took a few steps toward Kitty, studying her closely. "I believe I have seen you before, have I not? Were you not in the chapel one day some time ago with a Canadian officer?"

Surprised, Kitty nodded, recalling the day that she and Richard had gone there to pray.

"I thought so." Madame Rougeret smiled faintly. "I was in the back of the church that day and saw you come in. I prayed for you both."

"That was very kind of you, Madame."

"Well, what else can an old woman do in these terrible times? What can any of us do, really, but pray?" She sighed. "And your young man, he is all right?"

"Yes, thank God . . . so far."

"*Oui, très bien.*" Madame turned to go, then paused and gave Kitty a look of infinite pity. "*Pauvre petite.*" She shook her head sadly and walked slowly away.

chapter
20

"KITTY, WAKE UP!" Dora's urgent voice penetrated Kitty's drugged-like slumber.

Having fallen into bed after fifteen straight hours on duty, she resisted being awakened like this, but Dora's fingers dug into her shoulders, shaking her insistently. "Come on, old girl. This is an emergency!"

Kitty dragged herself to a sitting position. "What is it, Dora? Why are you waking me? I just got to bed—"

Dora sat down on the edge of the cot and caught Kitty just as she was about to drop back onto the pillows. "It's Richard! I'm sorry to have to break the news this way. But he's been badly wounded. I knew you'd want to know, be with him—"

Instantly Kitty was awake. "How bad is he?"

"Pretty bad. They're evaluating him now."

Dazed, Kitty stumbled out of bed and stood swaying with fatigue.

Dora steadied her, then handed her her dress and apron. "Here, I'll help you." Then, kneeling down in front of her as Kitty tugged on her stockings, Dora shoved each foot into the high-top black shoes, and began to lace and tie them.

When Kitty was on her feet, Dora studied her face. "You all right?"

"I think so—" Richard was here, wounded. She must get to him.

"I'm right behind you, Kitty. Let's go." Dora helped her out to the corridor, down the two flights of stairs, and into the pre-op ward.

Kitty had expected to see Dr. Marchand, but it was one of the British doctors, Captain Hayford, bending over the stretcher where Richard lay, making a preliminary examination. Bracing herself for the worst, Kitty clenched her hands and took her place beside the assisting nurse. This was the crucial point for any wounded man. Here the doctor made the decision to operate or . . . if it was hopeless . . . to allow the man to die in as much comfort as possible.

A nurse with a clipboard stood by, ready to jot down his orders.

When Kitty stepped up, the doctor gave her a quick glance before he dictated his diagnosis. "Hit in the lower lumbar section. Hard to say how many vertebrae may be involved . . . no movement . . . no feeling in lower extremities. Probable paralysis." He straightened and looked Kitty in the eye. "He needs surgery, but it's too delicate a procedure to do here. If he lives through the night, we'll tag him for evacuation. Dr. Manston in London is the only one I know who can tackle this kind of operation."

Kitty looked at Richard's expressionless face, drained of color, his handsome features pinched. She tried to see the man lying on the stretcher as she would have viewed any other wounded soldier. But it was *Richard!*

"We've shot him full of morphine." The doctor turned his attention to the recording nurse. "Keep him immobilized in splints and heavily sedated. That's all we can do for now."

Kitty cleared her throat as the doctor turned away to move

on to the next man. "Permission requested to remain on special duty with Captain Traherne, sir."

"Captain Traherne?"

"The wounded man, sir."

The doctor frowned. "You know him?"

Kitty swallowed. "He's my . . . we're engaged, sir."

The doctor's face remained impassive, but there was a flicker in the steely gray eyes. "What you're asking is highly unusual, Nurse. Not recommended at all!" he snapped but hesitated. "But it will have to be Matron's decision." With that, he moved on.

Kitty's request was quickly granted by the matron with the promise of authorization papers allowing her to accompany Richard to England, and she remained at his bedside most of the night.

It had been established that Richard had sustained trauma to his central nervous system, so he was heavily sedated to prevent further injury to his spine. Kitty learned that his legs were paralyzed, at least temporarily. The success of an operation to restore their use was an unknown at this time.

Reading his chart, Kitty knew his condition was poor, his prognosis negative. There was barely a chance that Richard would live at all, much less survive the trip to England.

By morning, when Richard's condition was unchanged and it was decided to chance the evacuation, Kitty left him long enough to pack a few things and change into her traveling uniform for the trip to Calais. From there they would board a steamer for England.

When she returned to the main floor, Dr. Hayford beckoned her into his office directly off the ward and handed her a small leather carrying case. Its lid was open to display several small vials of clear liquid, a syringe, and some hypodermic needles.

"Use these at your discretion, Nurse. I cannot overemphasize the necessity of keeping the patient as immobile as possible. Any movement might bring on a seizure or muscle spasm that could injure him fatally." The doctor speared her with his eyes. "The object is to keep him still, not to keep him entirely free from pain. He is anesthetized as much as is safe. When he wakes, he may beg for relief. I do not need to tell you that morphine is a very potent drug—" He halted abruptly, breaking off his thought. He closed the case and handed it to Kitty. "Administering this drug in proper amounts is critical, Nurse Cameron. I hope you're up to it."

His warning was clear. It would be imperative that she maintain professional distance and not give way to natural sympathy. She returned his steady gaze without wavering. "Yes, Doctor."

When Kitty entered Richard's ward to supervise his move to the ambulance, he was wrapped in bandages like an Egyptian mummy. His head was held rigid by splints on either side, his body tucked tightly into blankets, then buckled by canvas belts to restrict his movements.

Dora helped them out to the waiting ambulance. Once Richard was on board, she gave Kitty a fierce hug. "We'll all be praying. I know everything will be all right."

The ambulance jolted its way down the hill, Kitty wincing with each bump. Glancing at Richard, she was relieved to see that he was still too deeply sedated to feel anything.

Out the back window of the vehicle, Kitty glimpsed the charming little restaurant where Richard had told her he loved her and asked her to marry him. It was hard to believe that was only a few short months ago.

Huddled beside Richard's stretcher as the ambulance made

its way over the shell-pocked road, Kitty prayed desperately. "Please, God, please," she begged from between tightly clenched lips. She had been taught that it was wrong to bargain with God, but she couldn't help it.

The hours passed in a haze of unreality. From time to time, Richard moaned. His eyelids fluttered, but still he did not awaken. Fearfully Kitty took his pulse, counted his respiration. How much morphine had they given him? It was such a dangerous drug, often lethal—a blessing to those in agony, but also a curse, for it could be addictive.

It was dark when they reached the dock where Richard was to be carried aboard the ship to begin the treacherous Channel crossing.

Muscles aching, weary from the constant strain of watching over him so intently, Kitty got stiffly out of the ambulance to supervise Richard's unloading. "Careful now, please!" she cautioned the two orderlies who grabbed the handles of the stretcher and lifted it clear, then shifted to begin their awkward progress up the gangplank.

The sudden movement brought Richard to consciousness. When he cried out, Kitty leaned over him. "I'm here, Richard, dear. We're on our way to England. It will be just a little longer, then they'll take good care of you, make you well. Just hold on, dear."

They maneuvered up the narrow gangplank and onto the deck, Kitty walking beside him. On board, while there was a discussion of the cabin they would occupy during the voyage, Richard began to moan. His eyes, though glazed, roamed wildly. His face was contorted with pain. His breath came in short gasps.

Kitty got out the small leather case containing the vials of morphine. Her fingers fumbled with the buckles. By the time she got out the hypodermic needle, her hands were steady.

Just as she was about to draw sterilized water into the syringe, a voice spoke beside her.

"Why don't you do the poor bloke a favor and put 'im out of 'is misery?"

Kitty jerked about to see a British infantryman with a corporal's chevron on his uniform sleeve. A second look revealed that he was on crutches, one trouser leg pinned up. An amputee. Having assisted in many such operations, Kitty recognized the sarcasm, understood the bitterness.

"But he's going to have an operation," she replied quietly. "He's got a good chance of recovery if he can make it to England."

"Ha!" grunted the man. "Then wot kinda life 'as 'e got, I arsk ya? Look at me, will ya? I drove a lorry in civilian life and after I got in the Army. Then, one day we wuz drivin' down a road and . . . Pow! . . . it's Good-night, Irene, for me! Wot kinda job is there for a one-legged man? Not drivin' no vehicle! I might as well 'ave been blown up in me lorry," he said acidly, stumping off across the deck.

Richard moaned again, louder. Kitty turned to him, reminding herself of Dr. Hayford's warning. Biting her lip nervously, she dropped the correct number of tablets into the syringe. She rolled up his sleeve, swabbed his arm with alcohol, positioned the needle, and pushed down the plunger. Gradually his moans lessened as the drug brought merciful oblivion.

When the problem with the cabin was settled, two corpsmen came to move Richard, stowing him as gently as possible in the lower bunk. Kitty pulled a blanket and pillow from the top bunk and settled herself on the floor beside him to take up her vigil.

Looking at Richard's face, the lines of pain erased by the drug, Kitty was filled with compassion. This was the man she had promised to marry, the man who had promised to love and care for her for the rest of their lives. If he lived, it was far more likely that it would be she who would be doing the caretaking.

But there was no resentment in that thought, nor any self-pity. During that long night a strange and beautiful thing happened as she kept watch by Richard's side. The love she had not been sure of, the commitment she had not quite been ready to make, became a reality. This was the love freely given, the love that would endure "for better or worse, in sickness or in health."

"Oh, Richard, my darling," she murmured, resting her head on the wooden slat of the bunk, "I do take you now until death do us part."

They docked in the fog-shrouded early morning and were taken by ambulance to the train station where they boarded the train for London. There, at the private hospital of the recommended surgeon, Richard was to be examined. Then it would be decided whether he could undergo the operation that might enable him to walk again.

The London streets seemed very different this time. No flag-waving, cheering crowds lined the sidewalks. None of the glitter or glory. Four years of war had drained the country of the optimism she had observed in the people then as they embarked on what was to be a short war, "over by Christmas."

Richard's eyelids stirred, slowly opened. He moistened his parched lips with his tongue. Gradually his dulled eyes focused on her, then a glimmer of recognition came into them. "Kitty, love," he rasped.

A sharp, wild hope sped through Kitty. He knew her! He was going to be all right! He would get well! *Thank God! Oh, thank You, God!*

chapter
21

There's a long, long trail awinding unto the land
of my dreams,
Where the nightingale is singing, and the white moon beams.
There's a long, long time of waiting until my dreams
all come true,
Till the day when I'll be going down that long, long trail
with you.

THE SONG THAT had been so popular early in the war played over and over in Kitty's mind as she left Richard at the London hospital to return to France. He was in good hands. Although the operation had been a surgical success, it was uncertain whether or not he would ever regain the use of his legs. Only time would tell.

Please, God, please was the only prayer Kitty could manage. Everything felt unreal to her as she retraced the route she had taken nearly two years ago. The Channel crossing, the jolting bus ride back to Chateau Rougeret hospital were endured in a kind of trance-like state.

She had asked for and received an extended leave to see Richard through the surgery and the critical post-operative days. She had even briefly considered resigning so that she could stay with Richard and nurse him herself. But in the end, her sense of duty, knowing the acute need for nurses at the chateau hospital, would not allow her to do so.

All the way on the train from London, Kitty thought back over their last conversation before she left. She had gone into Richard's hospital room to say good-bye, and he'd taken her hand:

"Kitty, I want you to know I don't hold you to any promise you made . . . before this happened. You aren't under any obligation to me."

"Hush, Richard, don't say things like that. Don't even think them," Kitty had admonished, placing her fingertips on his mouth.

"Kitty, I mean it. There's no way of knowing how I'm going to come out of this. And I don't want you . . . wouldn't want anyone . . . tied to a man . . . who's no longer a real man."

"Richard, you're the man I love, the most real man I know, the bravest, the most—"

"Kitty, promise me . . . when the doctors give me the final outcome on all this . . . if it's negative—" He had halted. "You know I may never walk again—"

Glimpsing her reflection in the train window, Kitty hoped with all her heart that her expression had not betrayed her like this at Richard's bedside. As a nurse she had seen enough, learned enough in her experience to know that Richard's prognosis was not optimistic.

But it didn't matter. It wouldn't change her love, her loyalty to him. She thought of the day they had slipped into the little chateau chapel. In retrospect, their prayer, their pledge seemed as meaningful, as binding as the betrothal ceremonies of olden times. Whatever happened, she would never desert Richard, never renege on the promise she had freely given him.

*   *   *

November 1918

Kitty was in the small annex off her ward, writing one of the letters that had become her bittersweet duty in her assignment on the Salle de Mort, when news came of the armistice.

"Cameron, it's over! The war's over!" announced one of the VADs over the wild clanging of the chapel bell. "The Germans have surrendered. Come on out to the staff room and celebrate with us! Hurry up!"

Kitty let her go. As if from a long distance, she heard the sound of excited voices, the shouts, the rush of running feet along the stone corridors. Oddly, she felt nothing.

Of course, she was glad it was over—relieved that there would be no more killing, no mutilated bodies, no crippling wounds. But it would never be over for some. Not for Mrs. Benson to whom Kitty was finishing a letter about her son Bill. Kitty blinked back tears.

And it wasn't over for Richard. Or for her. They still had a long way to go. "There's a long, long trail awinding—" The refrain spun into her mind once more. Kitty straightened her shoulders and, with a sigh, continued writing.

After that, things happened quickly. By the end of the week all the VADs had been dismissed, for the hospital would soon be evacuated and closed. French nurses would take over the patient care, and all others would be sent home, to England and America.

The last day, Dora and Kitty packed up their belongings in the crowded little room they had shared for almost two years. Together, they went down the winding stone steps and gathered with the other members of the staff. The head French doctor and Matron each said a few words, commending the VADs for their excellent work. There was much shaking of hands, kissing, and hugging before the English VADs, Kitty with them, boarded the bus and departed for the two-hour trip to Calais for the Channel crossing.

Dora's family was waiting on the dock to greet her, and Kitty was introduced all around. She and Dora exchanged addresses, said a tearful good-bye, and Dora went off with her proud Mum and Dad. Kitty took the train up to London . . . and Richard.

Mayfield, Virginia
Fall 1919

There's a silver lining,
Through the dark clouds shining . . .
When our boys come home.
—a popular song of World War I

CARA CAMERON BRANDT stood on the terrace of Cameron Hall and breathed deeply of the crisp autumn air. Lines of a poem she had memorized as a child came to mind, something about purple gentians, sunshine, and "October's bright blue weather." She was suddenly happy in a way that she had not been happy in a long time.

Once in a sermon Owen had tried to explain the difference between joy and contentment. Then she had not really understood. She did know, however, that what she was feeling now was pure, lighthearted joy. It had nothing to do with loving Owen or their life together that was so earnest and so worthwhile and, yes, sanctifying.

She walked down to the stables and greeted the groom who had brought out her horse, Valor. Cara mounted, and the old spark of excitement stirred. It had been ages since she had been off for an afternoon's canter on a fine horse.

The air was sharp with the tang of autumn. The horse's ear twitched and he tugged at the reins, eager to take the stone fence at the end of the meadow.

A rush of remembrance coursed through Cara. She threw back her head and laughed, letting the reins slide forward in her hands, giving the horse his head.

She had not gone far along the bridle path when she heard the sound of hoofbeats. She reined sharply, listening, then turned in her saddle to see a man on horseback.

Kip! Kip Montrose. She had not seen him in five years.

As he came in sight of her, he drew up short, sending his horse rearing and tossing his mane. He circled, then leaning forward to calm his mount, Kip looked at her. An expression of disbelief crossed his face.

"Cara! Is it really you? I thought I was having some sort of delusion."

She laughed. "No, Kip, it's me."

He walked his horse nearer so they were side by side.

"How are you, Kip?" Cara asked, thinking he looked older, his eyes haunted. "I didn't know you were back."

"I didn't let anyone know I was coming."

"Didn't want a hero's welcome, eh?"

"Are there any heroes?"

She thought of Owen, who had given his life for someone he didn't even know. "A few."

Kip looked stricken. "I'm sorry, Cara. I didn't mean . . . He was a fine, fine man." He halted, frowning. "You're looking well, Cara. Are you here to stay?"

"No, just to see my parents. Actually, I'm going back to

France. I have a job in an orphanage there." She sighed. "There are so many orphans—" Her voice trailed away as she leaned down and patted her horse's bronze mane. "Somehow, I thought that going back, doing something to help might make it all seem worthwhile, after all."

Kip did not say anything. What was there to say?

"The truth is, Kip, this isn't home anymore. I've changed. I don't seem to belong here."

"I know what you mean. I'm not sure I do, either."

Cara smiled ruefully. "Perhaps *we* are casualties of the war, as well."

Kip looked straight ahead for a moment then turned and looked at Cara. "Everyone blames everything on the war— with justification in many cases. It *did* change things, changed the way people look at life. And it changed people. I suppose none of us will ever be the same."

Cara was surprised. This didn't sound like the old Kip. That Kip had rarely had such introspection. But then, he was right. The war had changed everyone.

"Well, I must go now. Mama will be wondering where I've been so long. I'm leaving in the morning. First, to Washington, D.C., to get all my papers in order, then to New York. I sail on the eighteenth of this month." She untied the horse's reins and hesitated, not knowing quite what to say. "I'm sorry about Etienette, Kip—"

There was nothing else to say. No word of sympathy or comfort would help, she knew too well. For both of them, there was a grave "somewhere in France" where all their young hopes and passions were buried.

Kip watched Cara go as horse and rider disappeared through the thick autumn woods. He had meant to ask her when Kitty was coming home, but being with the new Cara, the woman she had become, had distracted him. The girl he had once thought he loved had vanished, and it had shaken him.

His world, the one he'd missed and longed for, hoped to bring Etienette back to, was gone. He was left adrift. Maybe when Kitty came, he could get his bearings again—

chapter

23

Washington, D.C.

October 1919

THE MORNING she was to leave for Virginia, Kitty went out to see Richard at the hospital. Although the visit on the whole was cheerful, when it came time for her to leave she was aware of his mounting anxiety.

Checking her watch, she finally had to say, "I'll have to be going, Richard. Scott is treating me to lunch at some fancy Washington restaurant before taking me to the train." She got to her feet, leaned down to kiss him good-bye.

He looked up at her with those truth-seeking eyes. "Are you sure, Kitty?"

"Of course, I'm sure. I can't wait for you to see Mayfield, to meet my parents. And to show you our little house. It will be all snug and cozy, ready and waiting for you when they release you."

She kissed him then, and he drew her face down to his once more. "I love you."

"And I love you—" She smiled at him—"very much."

Scott met her at the entrance of the smart Georgetown

restaurant where he had made reservations for them. It was unadvertised but well-known and patronized by an elite clientele. A dignified headwaiter showed them to a table for two in the corner.

Everything was muted—the soft colors, the carpeted floor, the pearl-gray walls, even the lowered voices of the other luncheon guests. Kitty felt almost as if she should whisper.

"How was Richard?" Scott asked after he had ordered for them and handed back the oversized menus to their waiter.

"Better, I think. His spirits are good." Kitty tried to sound optimistic.

Scott leaned forward, looking at his sister earnestly. "This marriage is ill-advised, Kitty. You'll be marrying an invalid, you know, a desperately sick man who will never be able to give you what you've always wanted—a home, real love, children—"

"Scott, please. My mind is made up. It's what I want to do. I love Richard and he loves me . . . he *needs* me—"

"That's just it. Isn't it his condition that is motivating you to sacrifice yourself? Don't let sympathy or pity drive you to do something you may both regret."

"I'm not sacrificing myself. It's not as though either of us is being *forced* to do anything. We knew each other, fell in love *before* Richard was wounded, remember? That hasn't changed."

"But so much *has* changed. If you can't see that, you're being deliberately blind."

"You're wrong, Scott. Richard and I have so much in common. We understand each other."

Scott was silent for a minute as if considering something he wanted to say. "Kitty, let's be honest. You fell in love with Richard . . . or *thought* you did . . . *after* Kip—" Scott hesitated. "You know Kip is free again, don't you? That has to

206

make a difference. Don't let some mistaken sense of honor or loyalty bind you to Richard now. Surely he, as *any* man in his situation would understand, would want you to—"

Kitty's heart wrenched at her brother's words. Just then the waiter came with their soup, and neither of them spoke while it was placed before them.

When the waiter left, Kitty leaned forward, speaking in a low voice. "It doesn't matter, Scott. I'm going to marry Richard. Please let's not discuss it any more." She picked up her spoon. "Umm, this smells delicious."

But Scott made one more try. "What about Cara? What does she think of this?"

"Cara understands." Kitty smiled, thinking her twin was the only one who did. "Now are we finished talking about this?"

"I tried to talk *her* out of going overseas again." Scott shook his head, lifted an eyebrow. "But she didn't listen to me any more than you have."

"Dear Scott. You mean well, and we *do* appreciate all your brotherly concern for us, but we're grown women now, you know. You have to let us go, make our own mistakes if that's what we're doing. I really and truly believe that both of us have made the right choices."

"I hope so," Scott said doubtfully, unwilling to concede that his little sisters were adults now.

At the train station he thrust a box of chocolate-covered mints and a newspaper at her before seeing her to her seat.

"You will be at the wedding, won't you?" Kitty asked as Scott kissed her cheek.

He gave her a long look. "Of course. It wouldn't be official if I weren't."

Settled in her compartment as the train slid smoothly along the tracks from the station, out past the city toward Virginia,

Kitty recalled their conversation at lunch. She knew her brother's love and concern for her had prompted his words, wise and logical as they were. And he was partly right. Whenever she had dreamed of marriage, she had always thought of passionate love—what she had once felt for Kip Montrose. To be honest, she had never imagined caring for a disabled husband, one permanently crippled and confined to a wheelchair.

Yet Kitty knew she did love Richard. Maybe not the head-over-heels passion of her youth but with a deep caring and commitment. After all, she and Richard had been through a war together, had been tempered by loss, strengthened by surviving the unbearable. Their bond was deeper than perhaps anyone else could understand.

In that dark time after Kip's letter telling her he was going to marry Etienette, Richard had given her back a part of herself she thought was lost. When she had needed someone badly, he had been there. By loving her, he had restored her shattered confidence, given her something to live for. Scott simply did not know how much she owed Richard. But Kitty knew, and she was willing to pay that debt, if it took the rest of her life.

She stared out the train window. The landscape was growing more familiar as the miles rolled by. Richard loved her, needed her, and they were going to start a new life together, supporting each other, strengthening each other, giving to each other.

No doubt some lingering hurt might haunt her when she returned to Eden Cottage, but she was determined not to let memories of what might have been with Kip spoil the life she would share with Richard. It was going to be a good life, a good marriage.

After her broken engagement, Kitty had thought of Eden Cottage as described in a line from a poem by Tennyson:

Make me a cottage in the vale,
Where I may mourn and pray.

That quotation no longer applied. *It will not be a place of mourning,* she resolved to herself. *We'll be happy there. We will!*

Several days after her arrival at Cameron Hall, Kitty packed up the boxes of household goods and other belongings she was taking over to Eden Cottage. As she came downstairs from the bedroom she had shared with Cara, carrying a large cardboard carton, her mother was standing in the lower hall.

"Is that the last?" Blythe asked.

"Except for a few odds and ends of mine," Kitty replied, setting the box down beside several others near the front door.

"You've been working awfully hard, darling. Is it almost finished?"

"Oh, there are a few last-minute touches, of course. For one thing, I want to fill the house with flowers before Richard arrives. But I'll do that tomorrow."

Blythe gave her daughter a long, thoughtful look. "I hope you're doing the right thing, dear."

"Now, Mama, don't *you* start in on me." Kitty came over and put her arms around her mother. "Believe me, this is the right thing. You'll see."

"All I want is your happiness."

"I know, Mama, I love Richard, and we're going to be *very* happy," she assured her mother, and gave her another hug. "Now, I've got to go. I have lots to do. I'll just carry these out to the car and be on my way."

Upon her return to Virginia, Kitty had acquired a small station wagon. The dealer had made necessary adjustments to accommodate a wheelchair in the back. Now she filled the empty space with her boxes, got into the driver's seat, and drove down the curving drive to the gates.

After Kip and Kitty's engagement, when Eden Cottage was being renovated for their occupancy, their fathers had commissioned the construction of a road beginning where the Montrose and Cameron property lines converged. This had made the little house accessible from the county road.

As Kitty made the turn into the narrow lane leading to Eden Cottage, she caught sight of Montclair, viewing it through the foliage now tinged with the first colors of autumn. The Montrose home, like Cameron Hall, had been built in the early eighteenth century but retained an imperishable beauty. These two were among the few houses in the area still occupied by the same family who had built them, in spite of so many changes in the world.

Kitty slowed the car to gaze at it, thinking how many memories both great houses must hold—all the arrivals and farewells, the births and deaths, the christenings and funerals, the trials and triumphs of each generation. Yet both remained as a symbol of the strength of family love and loyalty and endurance.

It was thrilling to be a part of it. Kitty couldn't wait to introduce Richard to all that was hers, the heritage she might have failed to appreciate fully before the war.

She parked the station wagon at the side of the house where the sloping ramp had recently been built to accommodate Richard's wheelchair. She got out and stood for a moment, breathing in the familiar, indescribable smells of the woodland—the tree bark, pine needles, the spicy scent of marigolds and shaggy chrysanthemums along the low stone wall.

It was a glorious day. A golden haze gilded the maple leaves and fired the dogwoods with touches of scarlet. The grapevines on the arbor were glistening clusters of ripe color— gold, purple, emerald.

Stepping up on the porch, Kitty took out her key, inserted it into the brass latch, and opened the door. It squeaked a little, and Kitty smiled. She had meant to bring some oil to ease the ancient hinges, but it had slipped her mind. Oh, well, next time. She was about to enter the house when someone called her name.

"Kitty?"

For a moment, she could not move. She knew that voice, and her heart began to hammer wildly. Very slowly she turned around.

Standing only a few yards away was Kip. He was in his riding clothes—worn tweed jacket, beige jodphurs, leather boots. The sun slanted through the trees and enveloped his tall figure in an aura of unreality.

Kitty put one hand on the door frame to steady herself, for she was trembling. "Hello, Kip."

He came forward, stood at the foot of the porch steps. "Kitty! It's really you! I wasn't sure. I saw Cara near here the other day, and I thought at first it might be—"

"No, she's gone."

"When did you come?"

"Last week." Kitty was surprised that her voice sounded so normal.

"What are you doing here?"

"Didn't you know? I'm going to live here. That is, Richard and I are." She paused, seeing his brows furrow in a puzzled frown. "You *did* know I was being married . . . to Richard Traherne, didn't you?"

He shook his head. "No, I mean, yes. I didn't realize—" He halted. "Father and Fiona are away, in Bermuda. I just got home myself. I haven't actually seen anyone, talked to anyone—" He paused again. "When is the wedding?"

"Saturday."

"That soon?"

She nodded.

"And you're going to live *here*? At Eden Cottage?"

There was so much emotion in his voice that Kitty's hand gripped the porch railing tightly. What did she hear in it? Shock? Disbelief? Regret?

"You *do* remember deeding the house to me, don't you, Kip?" she reminded him gently.

He shook his head as if to clear it. "That was before the war . . . so much has happened—" His voice broke. He bent his head, drew a circle with the toe of one boot in the gravel path.

Kitty knew he was remembering more than that.

A silence fell. It was suddenly so quiet that the buzzing of bees among the flowers along the side of the porch droned loudly. Kitty stiffened.

Finally Kip raised his head and looked at her. "Let's take a walk. I think we should talk."

Kitty hesitated. Was it wise? What would they talk about— the past, old times, what might have been? Recalling them could only bring back the bittersweet memories, the anguish of their break-up, but would not change anything. She remained where she was until Kip held out a hand to her.

"Please, Kitty?"

She had never been able to refuse Kip anything. The pleading in his eyes drew her now, against her better judgment.

She ignored his hand, thrust both hers into the pockets of her sweater, and stepped down from the porch. They started down the walk along the pine-needled path leading down to the brook that eventually ran to the river.

"You know Etienette is dead." Kip spoke quietly, matter-of-factly.

"Yes. I'm sorry."

"I have a son. Her parents are keeping him until he's old enough for me to bring him home to Virginia. His name is Lucien."

Kitty said nothing. What was there to say in the face of the tragedy Kip had suffered?

"A lot of people died . . . young people, like Etienette . . . most of my friends in the Escadrille. I never told you, but the average life of a flyer was three weeks." When Kip spoke again, his tone was charged with irony. "We were lucky, Kitty, you and I. At least, I guess we were."

They walked on a little farther.

"When Etienette died, I didn't want to go on living. Then an old priest, the parish priest in the little village where she lived, the same one who married us, actually, said something I've tried to hold onto. He said that the Lord had left me here for some purpose. Most people never know why they're in this world. But he told me that since I have a son, maybe my purpose is to teach him that war is madness, that I should bring him up to be the kind of man who'll help the world learn that lesson."

Kip stopped abruptly and turned to face Kitty. "I could see what he meant. That's what I plan to do. Why I wanted to come back here, to Virginia, to Montclair, to my roots. I mean to bring Luc up with the values and traditions our families have held onto all these years." He paused, studying

213

her face intently. "I'd hoped to have some help doing that, Kitty."

He let the words hang between them, but their meaning was unmistakable. And when she looked into his eyes, she saw in them what she had always longed to see there—love, longing, need. Suddenly Kitty was aware of the danger they were in, and she was frightened.

What did she really want from Kip? Did she want him to say he was sorry, that marrying Etienette had been a mistake, that he wanted to pick up with Kitty where they had left off, just as if nothing had happened in all the years in between?

It was tempting to read into all of this what she might have wanted months ago. But if she allowed Kip to say what she sensed he was on the brink of saying and she listened— She halted suddenly, saying, "We'd better turn back."

"Wait, Kitty." Kip caught her arm, "There's something I have to say."

"Maybe it would be better not to say it, Kip."

"But I should have said it before," Kip insisted. "I wasn't too sensitive, was I? I've always been impulsive, thought-less—I didn't realize at the time—how much—"

"It's all right, Kip. I suppose we've both learned a lot, to appreciate happiness now more than we did before the war."

"That's not all I wanted to say, Kitty—"

Kitty knew that they were on dangerous ground and she interrupted him.

"It was a long time ago, Kip, no need to—"

"I *am* sorry, Kitty. Truly sorry."

Did Kip just mean sorry that he had hurt her or did he mean more than that? If she looked into Kip's eyes, what would she really see? Simply loss and loneliness or really love? Kitty dared not look. Instead she turned away, saying softly, "I must go, it's late, Kip."

"You mean that it's too late, don't you, Kitty?" she heard him say as she started down the path leading back to Eden Cottage.

He fell in step with her, and they walked the rest of the way in silence.

At the small herb garden, a miniature of the one at Montclair planted by the first Montrose bride, Noramary, Kitty bent and plucked a sprig of rosemary, held it for a moment, then handed it to Kip. "Rosemary for remembrance. Let's just remember the happy times."

They were standing close together, and he put his hand on her shoulder, letting it rest there for a moment, then leaned down and kissed her tenderly.

"I hope you'll be happy, Kitty. You deserve it."

Watching him walk slowly away, Kitty knew in her heart that she needed only to call his name to recapture her once-cherished dream. Then she glanced at the little house. It had a waiting look.

With an awful certainty Kitty realized that a step in either direction would change her life irrevocably. Was there a choice? Had life really handed her a second chance? The longing of the moment seemed irresistible. Or would there be an eternity of regret? The wind rustled the boughs in the tall pines overhead, making a sighing sound. Kitty shivered slightly, then she stepped out of the shadows and into the sunshine.

Cast of Characters for *Hero's Bride*

Mayfield, Virginia

Kip Montrose
Kitty Cameron
Cara (Kitty's twin)
Blythe and Rod Cameron (the twins' parents)
Lynette Montrose (the twins' grandparents)

In England

Lydia Ainsley (an old family friend)
Garnet Cameron Devlin (Kitty's aunt)
Bryanne Montrose (Garnet's granddaughter,
     Kitty's cousin)
Richard Trahern (a Canadian officer)
Scott Cameron (Kitty's brother)

The Brides of Montclair Series

. . . is a sweeping saga of a single American family, from before the Revolutionary War to the twentieth century. The twelve volumes are:

1. *Valiant Bride*
"If you enjoy reading romances, you'll enjoy reading *Valiant Bride*"—*Jane Mouttet, book reviewer, KHAC radio*

2. *Ransomed Bride*
"Earns a rousing A+"—*The Bookshelf WBRG*

3. *Fortune's Bride*
"Excellent . . . another triumph for Jane Peart!"—*Christian Readers Review*

4. *Folly's Bride*
This is the stunning "prequel" to Jane Peart's Civil War epic, *Yankee Bride/Rebel Bride*.

5. *Yankee Bride/Rebel Bride: Montclair Divided*
This novel is a newly revised expansion of the book that won the 1985 *Romantic Times* Award for Best Historical Fiction.

6. *Gallant Bride*
"Such a splendid book!"—a reader in Ontario, Canada

7. *Shadow Bride*
A continuation of the story of Blythe Dorman (many readers' favorite Jane Peart heroine) and her struggle to find lasting happiness.

8. *Destiny's Bride*
Druscilla Montrose finds love unexpectedly among the sun-drenched hills of nineteenth-century Italy.

9. *Jubilee Bride*
A Cameron and Montrose family reunion amid all the joy and romance of Victorian England.

10. *Mirror Bride*
Twins—alike yet not alike—search for their hearts' desires.

11. *Hero's Bride*
A novel of epic faith and endurance during World War I.

12. *Senator's Bride*
Love, politics, and abiding faith in the restless era "between-the-wars." (Due spring 1994.)